HOUSE OF CARDS

PORTH EWAN BAY

GARRETT LEIGH

2016 editing: Caz @ Riptide Publishing

Cover Art: Garrett Leigh @ Black Jazz Design

Production: Annabelle Jacobs

AUTHOR NOTE

This **British** book was originally written and published in 2016. Despite the extensive rewrites for this second edition, it is still set in 2016, and at that time, preventative PrEP wasn't available on the NHS, not even for the partners of people living with HIV, *unless* they'd had a high risk exposure. And at the time, Truvada was the drug of choice in British sexual health clinics.

Thankfully, sexual health care in the UK is a fluid entity, and things today are markedly different. As I write this in 2024, people living with HIV can take one pill, once a day, if their immune system tolerates that particular regimen. However, this book remains true to its time.

And regarding the Rebel Kings, which I know will have brought a lot of you here, this is not a Rebel Kings book. There's no gang violence and murder, haha. But there are cameos, some glimpses of the past (if you've ever wondered where Saint got his tattoos…you might get a hint of it here), and *of course*, I've treated you to an iconic Rubi moment.

Thank you for being here and enjoying a trip back in time with me. Please heed the **trigger warnings** for HIV infection, depression, suicidal ideation, domestic violence, suicide/death of a relative, homophobia, gender identity trauma (*of a side character*), and chronic illness. This book is a heavy read at times, but I promise it's worth it for Brix and Calum's hard won happy ending.

Many thanks to Sadie for the double sensitivity read.

Garrett x

#iykyk

CHAPTER
ONE

LONDON

Calum Hardy dipped the needle into the black ink and pressed his foot to the pedal of Dottie, the faithful old-school coil machine he'd had since his apprenticeship in Camden. Rob kept telling him to upgrade to one of the shinier models on the market, but Calum wasn't about that life.

He liked the noise, and the weight of Dottie heavy in his hand. In a world where most things were slipping through his fingers, this felt real.

"I'm so nervous."

Calum blinked, refocusing on the client stretched out on the table. "That's normal. Just try not to tense up. It'll hurt less if you're relaxed."

The girl gave up a wan smile. "That's why I came to you. My friend told me you're gentle."

"I am, but it'll still hurt, so you have to see the needle for what it is. A tiny sliver of metal, and you're stronger than that."

"I guess."

Calum left the girl to her nerves and returned to the candy-skull stencil he'd already applied to her thigh. This moment was his and Dottie's.

He pressed the pedal again, waiting for the comforting buzz, but nothing happened. Then the lights went out, plunging the shop into darkness.

Power cut.

Great.

Third time that week.

Calum set the gun down and went to the front door of the shop. He glanced out into the street and caught the eye of the maintenance worker who'd been the bane of his life all week long.

The worker shrugged. "Sorry, mate. Give us an hour or so."

Nice of him to say, but it was already gone five. Candy-skull girl was Calum's last client of the day. Grumbling, he went back inside and gave her the news. She looked a little too relieved and left without rebooking.

With her gone, Calum lit a candle and cleaned up the shop, a job done by the receptionist in most studios, except Calum's receptionist was Rob's cousin, and she downed tools at four every day, taking no notice of Calum's protests.

Fuck my life.

Calum left the shop an hour later. Bought a cheeky bottle of rum and turned in the direction of home—a one-bedroom flat two streets away. He called Rob, but as usual, there was no answer. Rob only took Calum's calls when he wanted something. Shame, because with Calum at a loose end, they could've grabbed some dinner, a drink . . . maybe more. It had been a while since they'd had some quality time to themselves. Work, play, work again, there always seemed to be something keeping them apart.

The flat where Calum lived alone loomed into view. Rob was probably down the road in the Ship, drinking up a storm on the shop's expense account. Calum thought about joining him, then he remembered Rob's reaction the last time he'd dropped in on him uninvited and a dark shudder rippled through him.

Give him space, remember? Stop smothering him.

Damn.

When had loving someone become so complicated? All Calum wanted was a cuddle and a bag of chips.

He let himself into the flat, his mind stuck in the awkward space that came with contemplating his skewed relationship with Rob.

This is why you don't bother.

An empty mind was a happy one, right?

Wrong.

What a load of shit.

Calum dropped his keys in the bowl. His gaze fell on a pair of loafers by the kitchen door—Rob's latest fad—and beside them, a pair of chavvy Nikes that were too big for Rob.

And too big for me.

Calum frowned. Rob never came over when Calum wasn't there unless he needed cash from the kitchen drawer, and he never, *ever*, brought his mates round. God forbid; Calum was way too boring for Rob's clique of wankers who seemed to do nothing but snort coke and talk about fisting.

Voices drifted down the hallway—no words, just sounds that set Calum's teeth on edge, and his frown deepened. *Surely not.* Rob had been distracted lately, leading Calum to suspect he might have been—but *no* . . . not here. Rob wouldn't do *that*, would he?

There was only one way to find out. Calum steeled

himself and trod silently down the hallway to the bedroom. The door was ajar, and unless whoever was inside was watching some hard-core porn, what he'd find on the other side was already solidified in his brain, etched on his fucking soul.

But he did look. Calum *stared* at the tangled mess of flesh in his bed: sweat-sheened skin, curled toes, arched backs, and scraping nails. And you know what? In another world—one where the dude getting fucked by a six-foot beefcake wasn't his boyfriend—the scene playing out in his bedroom would've been hot. But there was nothing hot about watching Rob hammer the final nail into a relationship that had been wonky from the start.

There was nothing but twisted solace.

This is your chance. Kick him out.

If only he could make his feet move, and his brain compute what his heart had known for months. That this shit was toxic. That it was killing him. And if Calum didn't get out now, he'd die in this fucked up relationship.

He backed up, trying to tiptoe away as unnoticed as he'd arrived. Fuck everything. Fuck it all. He'd go to the shop and kip there. Come back when Rob went to work and change the locks.

He'll let me go this time.

But even as Calum thought it, he knew it wasn't true. How many times had Rob told him—warned him—not to step out of line?

I'll ruin you. You're nothing without me—

"Where the fuck do you think you're going?"

Calum froze, heart in his mouth, every instinct screaming at him to keep walking, but the masochist in him won out.

He turned to face Rob, who was still bent over the bed, his

brawny pal balls-deep inside him, and his face curled in a smirk that showed exactly how he felt about being caught.

I fucking hate him. Calum clenched his fists. "Doesn't seem like you need me here."

"You can suck my dick if you want."

"No, thanks."

Rob's hawkish gaze narrowed, belligerence morphing to anger. "Don't be a twat."

"Me?" Calum laughed, bitter and brutal. "I'm not the twat here, but tell you what. How about I leave you to it? That way it doesn't fucking matter."

He stepped back, spun on his heel, and ran for the door before Rob got close enough to give him that look—the one that always seemed to penetrate Calum's brain and extinguish any thoughts of his own. The one that Calum had never been able to hide from, ever since the first time he'd caught Rob out in a lie.

What do you expect when you're so uptight? I'm not flirting, I'm just blowing off steam."

Calum stumbled, his foot catching the bookcase in the hallway. He hit the wall, but footsteps behind him spurred him on.

Get out, get out, get out.

"Not so fast." A cool hand closed around Calum's wrist. "Don't walk away when I'm talking to you."

"Why not?" Calum wrenched his wrist. "Looks like you're managing fine without me."

Rob's grip tightened, *twisting.* "So? You're not even supposed to be here. You said you were working late."

Like that made it okay. "Power cut. I can't ink in the dark."

Rob smirked. "No?"

"Fuck off." The barely veiled derision made Calum's skin itch. Rob's name was on the lease of the shop, but though he had no problem spending the profits, belittling Calum's work had always been a hobby. That Black Star Ink was booked months in advance, with cancellations snapped up within seconds of announcement, meant nothing to him. "Does it matter where I'm supposed to be? Point is you're banging someone in my bed."

"Don't be so dramatic."

Calum shoved Rob's chest. "Get the fuck off me."

"Why? What are you going to do? Run to your mother or some shit? Grow *up*. It's just sex. You can watch if you don't want to join in." Rob stepped closer, bracing his hand on the wall, blocking Calum's escape route. "Come on, Cal. You know I love you. I just get a bit suffocated sometimes. He's just a friend. You want me to have friends, don't you?"

Calum had fallen for that speech more times than he cared to remember, and perhaps tonight would've been no different if *the friend* hadn't appeared in the bedroom doorway, wrapped in Calum's duvet and laughing his over-ripped arse off.

"I'm leaving," Calum ground out. "Get back on his dick. I'm done with this shit."

Rob made a grab for Calum's other arm, but Calum evaded. He got his knee between Rob's legs and shouldered his way free, wrenching his arm from Rob's grasp.

"Calum, stop it."

"No."

"*Calum.*"

The warning in Rob's tone prickled Calum's skin, but he didn't stop to let the weight of it reel him in. He ran for the door, Rob cursing behind him, and charged down the stairs

Outside, damp evening air hit him as he threw himself into the crowds of commuters flowing up the street to the nearby station. He'd made it to the coffeehouse on the corner when he heard his name again.

"Calum! Stop!"

No chance. Calum kept going, head bowed, shoulders stiff, until he came to the zebra crossing and the fast-moving London traffic forced him to make a choice between waiting and literal death.

"Calum."

"Fuck off." Calum didn't turn round. The traffic stopped. He strode across the road, dodging Rob's reaching hands.

"Stop."

"No."

"Calum!" Rob caught Calum's arm and dragged him off course, pulling him from the crowd and behind a nearby bus stop. "I said, stop."

"Get off me." Calum fought Rob's hold, lurching away. Rob lashed out and punched him in the face.

Bastard.

Calum's eyes watered, and he faltered long enough for Rob to grab his arm again and yank him back, slamming him into a nearby wall.

"Get a fucking grip. Where do you think you're going to go? The shop's in my name, remember? You bail on me, I'll shut it down."

"Do it." Calum fought Rob's hold on him and shoved him away. "I don't give a shit anymore."

Rob fell to the ground, drawing the attention of onlookers, like he always did when Calum found the balls to bite back, letting everyone know that his six-foot-three lover had laid a hand on his slighter frame. "You won't give up the shop. It's everything to you."

"It's nothing if it's got your name on it. I told you. I'm done."

"Done?" Rob laughed and scrambled to his feet, putting himself in Calum's face again. "Are you kidding me? Four years of your bullshit and you think *you're* going to walk out on *me*?"

"My bullshit? I'm not the one taking someone else's dick."

"Like you'd even know how. Like you'd even know how to *fuck me* if I asked you to. Have a day off, Calum. It's not like I screwed your best mate. I just needed something extra. Come on. We've talked about this. It's not my fault you only want to bottom."

Calum closed his eyes, fighting the poisoned logic that always swept over him when Rob got in his face. The logic that told him Rob could do whatever the fuck he wanted because he always came back to Calum in the end, put his arms around him, and said he loved him. The logic that *told him* Rob meant it, because no one would lie about that, right?

Another big fat *wrong*. "We didn't talk about it. You got wasted and decided I should fuck women so you'd have an excuse to get blown by every bloke who looked your way."

"And what's up with that? You like pussy, don't you?"

That Calum had been with women before Rob had always been a thing. *You're not really gay, though, are ya, Calum? You're not one of us.* "I don't want to fuck anyone else."

"Well maybe you should. Then you might be better at it."

In years—no, days—gone by, Rob's words would've cut deep, slashing Calum and what remained of his self-esteem to bits, but there was nothing left to break. He pushed Rob away again. "Fuck. You."

"Cal—"

"Fuck *off*."

Calum sidestepped Rob's reaching hands and kept moving. Behind him, Rob shouted, but Calum didn't stop. Didn't look round, didn't *breathe*, until the station swallowed him up, cocooning him in its humid warmth.

The respite was brief.

Calum's phone rang in his pocket, blaring out Rob's ringtone. He silenced it, but it rang again and again until he dumped it in a nearby bin.

He's going to follow me.

Calum jogged down the steps and ran for the nearest ticket machine. He stuck his debit card into the machine and jabbed at the screen until a ticket to who-the-fuck-knew-where printed out.

He snatched it and stumbled further into the station, waving it at a uniformed station worker.

She pointed ahead. "Platform eight. Hurry. It's leaving soon."

Heart in his throat, Calum dashed through the station. The ticket barriers appeared in the distance as someone yelled his name from behind. Calum ran harder, shoulder-barging past anyone in his way. Rob had an Oyster Card, the barriers wouldn't stop him, but they'd buy Calum precious time to make the train idling on the distant platform.

He crammed his ticket into the barrier slot and barged through the gates. Rob hollered again as the last-call alarms began to sound on the train that was still fifty feet away, and Calum gritted his teeth. *Goddamn it.* He'd make that fucking train if it killed him, because the alternative would do the same.

I'm done. So fucking done.

It felt as pathetic as it sounded. But Calum pushed harder, sprinting towards the platform, and he made the train with seconds to spare, stumbling on board as the doors closed behind him, snapping a sharp breeze over the back of his neck.

Head down, he sidestepped along the aisle, searching for a vacant seat. Something thumped the window, but he didn't react. Didn't blink until he found a seat and slumped into it, clenching his teeth against the surge of anxious adrenaline rushing up from his stomach.

Don't puke. Don't puke.

Damn. He needed a drink, a big one, a *strong* one, anything to quell the panic rising in his chest.

What have I done?

Rob wouldn't forgive this, even if Calum went back now, and he had Calum's whole life in his hands—the shop, the flat.

I've lost it all.

But as the train rumbled to life, eerie calm descended on him, like a guillotine had cut his desperation off at the neck.

I don't care.

And he didn't. All he wanted was peace . . . and quiet, and on the crowded train, with people all around, for the first time in years, he had it.

Wrecked, Calum rested his head against the cool glass and felt months of tension drain away. His messy brain told him he still loved Rob, but his heart was ominously silent. And it was the silence that held as the train began to move.

Half an hour passed before he remembered he didn't have a clue where it was going. The thought of crawling home to his parents sent a fresh wave of nausea rippling through his gut, but it felt inevitable. He'd always known that leaving Rob would send him to skid row.

You don't have to do this. Get off the train and go home.

He didn't. For the longest time, he closed his eyes.

Then he opened the bottle of rum.

CHAPTER
TWO

PORTH EWAN

"Peg, I don't give a shit how busy you are, I don't want them crates in my yard."

"'*Yard*'? Jesus Christ, boy. You've been out of London years now and you're still jabbering like a cockney?"

"Whatever. Get them gone."

Brix Lusmoore put the phone down before his infamous aunt ripped him a new one, and ran a frazzled hand through his too-long hair. How had the day become a shambles already? He'd barely woken up.

He dropped his phone on the kitchen counter and went to the window, eyeing the crates of counterfeit DVDs that had mysteriously appeared on his patio overnight, except there was no mystery in it at all. Peg always had her nose in a pie she shouldn't, and if she wasn't behind the shadowed delivery in his back garden, he'd eat his bloody hat.

Not that he had a hat. Brix rolled a bandana and tied it around his wayward hair. Early it might have been, but he had shit to do, and he hadn't eaten breakfast yet.

And the rest.

Brix gave the whispering demon the mental bird and tore himself from the window, drifting to the fridge to take his chances. Nothing inspired him, and the odd feeling he'd woken up with swept over him again—like the wind had changed and the sea had brought a message to shore.

Not hungry.

He'd pay for it later, but if he was going to get his rusty van to Truro in time to meet the farmer, he needed to leave.

He found the van keys beneath five kilos of corn, reminding him to feed the girls, and dump the sack in the shed before he left. Outside, he scattered pellets on the damp soil, watching the ballsy politics of his flock of rescued hens—a dozen or so, in all, but soon to be more if he could get his shit together enough to leave the house.

You can't be late.

Hustling, he climbed into the van reversed down the driveway, onto the street below. Porth Ewan roads were *narrow,* and despite knowing the town like the back of his hand, it took all his concentration to manoeuvre the van through the twists and turns until he hit the southbound A road.

Truro was a forty-minute drive on a good day. It seemed like he'd barely blinked when the sign for the small-scale commercial poultry farm came into view.

He made the turn and coaxed the van down the dirt track that led to the two huge barns. The farmer was waiting outside, leaning against his own truck, a stack of wooden crates to his left.

Brix pulled up and jumped out, the cash he needed already in hand. Experience had taught him that these transactions needed to be quick, before he wound up feeling guiltier than if he'd not come at all.

He waved a roll of notes at the farmer. "Bullseye, yeah?"

"Can give you another five if you slap a cockle on that."

Brix considered it. Fifty quid was already a lot for forty chickens heading to the slaughterhouse, and five for an extra tenner made them expensive per bird, but then, he wasn't buying them for their monetary value. "Sold. Load 'em up."

The farmer crammed five more chickens into cramped crates that were probably bigger than the cages they'd come from. Brix paid up, loaded the crates onto the van, and made his escape before the plaintive clucking of the doomed hens still on the farmer's truck reached his ears.

A little way from the farm, he pulled into a lay-by and retrieved his phone from the dashboard. He brought up the group message he'd set up the day before and typed in the postcode of the meeting place, then sent the message with a smirk. These meets reminded him of the warehouse parties in Brixton all those years ago, the ones that had no location until a van pulled up outside a disused factory and set up a rig. Oh, how life had changed.

Message sent, he set off again, heading for the quiet location where he'd meet the band of folk who were as soft-hearted as him.

Fifteen minutes later, he arrived at the deserted quarry. He parked up and got out of the van, opening the back doors to give the hens some air. His fingers itched for the cigarettes he'd quit a long time ago, a phantom tic he'd yet to shake. God, he missed a solitary smoke. Back then, a snatched cig had often felt like the only time he could breathe.

But it's different now, ain't it?

And it was. Life back home in Porth Ewan was as unique and familiar as it had ever been, and for the first time in years, Brix wouldn't change a thing . . . except one thing, maybe—

His phone rang in his hand. He jumped and studied the screen. *Peg*. Typically, she hung up after one ring, trusting that he'd call her back and foot the bill. And she was right.

Brix placed the call.

She picked up straightaway. "Ah, there you are, boy. I've been looking for yer all morning."

"Yeah? Where've you looked?"

Peg clicked her teeth. "That's enough of your cheek. You seen your dad?"

"Not since Monday. Why?"

"Ah, you know."

Peg spoke as if Brix was a fly on the wall to every hustle and scheme she had her sticky fingers in, but he resisted arguing. Reminding her a second time that he'd spent most of his life trying to avoid Lusmoore dodgy dealings would only set her off, and he didn't have time for a marathon rant today.

"I haven't seen him."

"Well if you do, tell 'im I've got his dosh here from the Kings. If he's not home by tea time for it, I'm having it for housekeeping."

Brix rolled his eyes. His father and Peg had been bickering for as long as he'd been alive. "He'll be on the boat till lunchtime. You know that. You moved those crates yet?"

"Lord, is that the time?"

"Peg, don't take the piss—"

"Now, you listen here, boy. Don't go giving me none of your lip. I'll fetch them later when I'm good'un ready and not a minute sooner. Tell yer dad to get his sorry behind home."

It was Peg's turn to hang up, leaving Brix shaking his head. Damn woman was a hornet's nest, and a royal pain in his arse, though her call had reminded him he was due a check in with hold man Lusmoore.

A vehicle rumbled up the dirt track to the quarry. Brix pocketed his phone and rounded the back of the van to take a look. Another car was behind it, and a Land Rover behind that. Game on. Fuck Peg's smuggled cigs and booze, counterfeit crap, and *Lord* knew what else; it was time to do God's work.

Brix waited until all eight recipients of his group message had assembled by the quarry, and then unloaded his precious cargo. "Okay, folks. Who's having what? I've got fifty girls here, all looking for forever homes."

A man who appeared even less like a chicken keeper than Brix raised his hand. "We're taking six."

Brix nodded. "Got room for an extra? Farmer gave me a few more than I was expecting."

"I'll take a couple, just don't tell the missus."

"Awesome." And so it went on. Brix rehomed forty-two hens, leaving him the five he'd committed to taking himself and three extra he'd need to place with whichever friends he hadn't already foisted rescued chooks on, which wasn't many. In fact, as he loaded the leftover birds and the crates onto the van, he couldn't think of anyone who'd have the room, no one except . . . *Aw, shit.* Perhaps he'd be seeing his father sooner than he'd planned.

Brix shut up shop, pocketing the nominal monies folk had paid for their chooks—barely enough to cover the fuel—and got back in the van. Damn thing stank of chicken shit, but the stench was worth even giving up his lucrative Saturday slot in the studio.

On cue, Brix's phone rang again, the number for Blood Rush lighting up the screen. He plugged in the rickety hands-free kit, then put the van in gear and reversed. "Yeah?"

"Sunshine. Did I wake you?"

"What do you think?"

Lena chuckled. "I think you've been up for hours, saving all the chickens in the world from the pot."

"Very funny." Brix hung a left. "How many of my girls have you got up at the commune?"

"Eighteen at last count, so don't try it."

"But—"

"I mean it. All the lectures in the world about commercial egg production won't give me any more room. You don't want the poor things stacked up worse than where they came from, do you?"

Of course he didn't, and she knew it. Brix sighed. He'd have to go home and make more space, and take what he couldn't house to his dad. "So if you haven't called to take extra girls off my hands, what do you want?"

"I called to see if you want me to fill your cancellation on Thursday. Some dude's coming all the way from London, so he wants a long sitting."

"All the way from the big smoke, eh? Surely he isn't coming just to get inked?"

"That's what he said. He nabbed your cancellation when I posted it first thing. Said the city studio he was booked at closed down overnight. Artist did a moonlight flit or something."

Fair enough. Brix was used to folk coming from all over to get inked at Blood Rush. He let his mind drift over the designs he'd compiled the night before, ready for the week ahead. "Is this the dot work you messaged me about at 5 a.m.?"

"The very same. I've priced it at four hours, so if you don't take too long on Cam, and you stay till six, you can wrap it up in one sitting."

Brix snorted. "It isn't me who spends too much time with Cam O'Brian."

Lena's dirty laugh filled the van. "Don't start a conversation you're not built for, my friend. Are you game for Thursday or not?"

Brix took the hint and agreed to everything Lena suggested, wondering for the umpteenth time how he'd manage without her. Lena was a knockout—neon haired, inked, and dangerous—and she ran Blood Rush so well he often joked that if she could do the ink herself he'd be out of a job. "What time is my afternoon appointment?"

"Two-thirty. Are you going to be late?"

"*Moi*?" Brix turned onto Truro's Station Road. "You say it like I'm late all the time."

"You are. I had to break into your house and pour a bucket of water on your head last week."

"Yeah, yeah." Brix had no defence. He hadn't even learned to tell time until he was twelve. Before then, he'd relied on the sun, just like his dad. Who needed a watch when you had nowhere to be?

Brix said goodbye and tossed the phone on the seat beside him. He turned the radio on and fiddled with the dial, searching for anything that didn't make him want to launch the stereo out of the window.

Porth Luck FM then.

Fuck, I'm getting old.

He set the pirate-rock track to a low volume as the van rumbled past the train station, the busiest in Cornwall. Brix was used to seeing all types of folk flow in and out of it on any day he happened to pass by, but as he crossed the bus entrance, a lone figure on a bench caught his attention. The man was slumped, hood up, with his head in his hands, and

Brix had never seen such a picture of abject misery. Not in someone else, anyway.

The van slowed, Brix's foot subconsciously easing off the accelerator. Something about the set of the dude's broad shoulders was familiar. Brix eased to a crawl as he passed the bench and then stared hard in the wing mirror. The man's hands were clenched into tense fists, but dark ink stained the tendons of his right hand, snaking out into an intricate web of black-and-grey Brix would recognise anywhere.

Jesus Christ, it can't be.

But it had to be, because the unique design was the first of its kind that Brix had ever done, etched onto the trembling hand of his gorgeous new apprentice eight years ago.

Eight years? Fuck. Where did the time go?

Brix shook his head—*I've got to be seeing things*—but he pulled up and jumped out of the van anyway. Whoever the raven-haired, bearded fittie was, he looked like he needed help. "You all right there, mate?"

The man didn't move. Brix ventured closer, his gaze drawn to the ink. The dots spread out over flawless skin, weaving an image Brix already knew—a stag, with its antlers wrapped around the index and little finger, strong and proud, interwoven with the delicate touch that made dot work so special.

It had aged well.

Brix reached the bench and knelt down, tracing the antlers with his fingertip. "Calum? Is that you?"

CHAPTER
THREE

"Calum? Mate?"

"Huh?" Calum raised his head and blinked at the latest apparition to cross his path since he'd fallen off a train at the bottom of the world.

Great.

Now he was imagining the first bloke he'd ever got a hard-on over. Would this nightmare never end?

Not that imagining Brix Lusmoore was much of a nightmare. Even in the midst of the clusterfuck Calum's life had become, Brix was beautiful.

Shame he wasn't real.

Calum let his gaze drop back to the wet concrete he'd been staring at since he'd discovered that Rob had cleared out their joint bank accounts, rendering his debit card—his *only* card—totally fucking useless. With no phone and no money, and nowhere to run, Calum was stranded.

And drunk.

Very drunk.

"Calum."

Brix's ghost spoke again. Calum ignored it as a phantom

hand, darkly inked with familiar pirate tattoos, closed around his, squeezing, shaking, and punctuating every utterance of his name.

"*Calum*. Dude. Anyone home?"

Nope. Even if Brix had been real, Calum definitely wasn't home, because home was where Rob was fucking someone else in his bed.

Bastard.

The ghost stood and disappeared. Calum mourned the loss of its warming touch. Then the world tilted and the phantom hand returned, grasping Calum's arm and hoisting it over a set of slim shoulders that were far too bony to be a dream. "Is it really you?"

"Depends who you think I am," Brix said. "If you call me Cunty-Bastard-Rob again, I'm gonna bloody deck you."

Cunty-Bastard-Rob. Calum let out a strangled laugh as the half litre of rum he'd drunk on the train threatened to make an abrupt reappearance. "Rob is a cunty bastard."

"I'm sure he is. Don't explain why you're all banged up and trashed on a broken bench, though, does it?"

Calum touched the bruise on his face and supposed it didn't, but though Brix had pointed out the wound, he didn't appear to be asking for an explanation. "What are *you* doing here? Thought you were dead or some shit."

"Close, mate, close. Been a long time, eh?"

"Yeah." Calum searched his rum-riddled mind for any clue as to exactly how long it had been since he'd last seen Brix Lusmoore, but as he stared at the blue-grey eyes he'd often seen in his dreams, he honestly had no idea. All he remembered was coming back to London one day to the news that Brix had packed his stuff from the flat he'd shared with a mutual friend and vanished. "Where've you been?"

"I've been right here, Cal."

Cal. Brix was the only soul on earth who'd ever been able to shorten Calum's name without making his teeth itch. "Here?"

"Yup."

Calum frowned, missing something—*years* of something—but his brain and mouth didn't feel connected, and his only response was a nonsensical grunt.

Brix didn't seem to notice, too preoccupied keeping Calum upright. The absurdity of the scene almost made Calum laugh again, but he didn't laugh. He stared, and as he accepted that Brix wasn't a hallucination of too much rum and not enough sleep, his equilibrium deserted him.

He lurched sideways, despite Brix's hold on him, and braced for impact, perversely craving it, like the pain of his bones slamming into the concrete would erase the sting of Rob's betrayal. But he didn't fall. Brix held firm, and as he guided Calum away from the bench to a nearby van, Calum realised that this was what he remembered most about Brix. Not his shaggy, dark-blond hair, awesome ink, or hypnotic gaze, but the subtle strength in his slender arms. Strength that had made Calum feel safe from the moment they'd met in London all those years ago.

Brix deposited Calum in the passenger seat of the battered van. "Where's your stuff?"

"What stuff?"

"Your things. You got a bag?"

"Nope."

"Okay." Brix tried again. "Are you with anyone? Someone you want me to call?"

Calum couldn't contain a humourless bark of laughter. "I

ain't gotta phone, Brixie, and even if I had, no fucker would care if you called."

"I don't believe that." Brix's frown was troubled. "Listen, I can't leave you by the side of the road in this state. How about you come back to mine for a shower and a kip?"

The only place Calum could remember Brix living was the Camden flat he'd abandoned. He shook his head, reeling at the dizziness that came next. "I'm not going back to London. Fuck that. I'll walk to my mum's."

"In Reading?"

"Sure. Why not?"

Calum started to get out of the van, but Brix pushed him back. "Don't be a dick. Man, I'd forgotten what a riot you are when you've been on the juice. Just come back to mine for a bit, yeah? It's half an hour away. I'll make you some coffee and we'll figure out whatever's got you in this mess."

"Mess?"

"Yeah. Cal, it's good to see you, but you look like hell."

Calum didn't doubt it, and lacking any brighter ideas, he pulled his legs back inside the van and clumsily shut the door.

Brix climbed in the other side and the van rumbled to life. Calum cast a lazy glance at his rescuer, absorbing his unshaven jaw, his elegant neck, and his *beautiful* coiled forearms. He'd always had a fetish for forearms, especially Brix Lusmoore's.

Again with the strength.

How had Calum forgotten that?

A years old urge to touch Brix swept over him, but it was eclipsed by an overwhelming need to close his eyes.

He gave in and shut the world out, and the darkness, combined with the gentle rolling of the van, and Brix's silent presence beside him, was so fucking good he almost moaned aloud. The noise in his brain quieted, but for one thing. "Brix?"

"Yeah?"

"Your van stinks of shit."

Consciousness returned to Calum slowly. Smells first—coffee and toast—and then sounds: a door opening and shutting, heavy metal music playing at a volume so low it was like a lullaby, and the gentle rumble of…a smug cat.

He opened his eyes to find himself under siege from a pair of moggies who couldn't have contrasted more if they'd been cat and dog.

One was tiny and digging a hole in his chest. The other was *massive*—like a panther who'd eaten all the pies—and without its booming purr, Calum would've been pretty disconcerted by its unblinking stare.

As it was, a giant cat was the least of his worries. Calum gazed around at the unfamiliar room, the wooden floors, the low beams, and the open fire. The squishy brown leather couch, the canvases stacked up in the corner, and pirate-themed artwork dotted around. The only thing he recognised was the empty bottle of rum on the coffee table, but its presence made as little sense as the rest of his surroundings. Last Calum knew, he'd dropped it on the floor of the train carriage.

Oh shit, the train.

Like a tidal wave, the events of the last twenty-four hours came rushing back. The power cut, heading home early . . . *Rob.* And then Calum's flight from the city, jumping on the first train he saw, drinking himself into a stupor, and sleeping like a dead man until he woke up in *fucking Cornwall.*

Damn.

The rest of it was sketchy, so much so Calum still half

believed he'd dreamed it, but on cue, the exterior door to what he was fast realising was a cosy cottage opened, and *Brix Lusmoore* appeared in Calum's bleary line of sight. "Shit. You're real."

"Shit, you're awake," Brix retorted. "I was beginning to think you'd drunk yourself into a coma."

The notion didn't feel that far from the truth, judging by Calum's headache, but as he swallowed the sour taste in his mouth, he was distracted by Brix wiping his feet on the door-mat. "Are you wearing wellies?"

Brix eyed Calum like he was the one who'd grown horns. "What of it?"

Calum opened his mouth, shut it again. He would've pictured Brix in ballet shoes first. "Erm . . . this might seem a strange question, but where am I?"

"It ain't that strange if the state of you this morning is anything to go by." Brix pulled his *wellies* off and left them outside, shutting the back door behind him. "Could hardly believe my eyes when I saw you huddled up on that bench. Woulda passed on by if I hadn't seen matey boy on your hand."

Calum twisted his hand to see the stag, so carefully etched all those years ago. He remembered it like it was yesterday, how pumped he'd been to get his first ink—by *Brix Lusmoore*, an artist Calum had idolised since he'd first come to London. Nearly a decade later, it was still his only tattoo.

"You're in Porth Ewan, by the way."

"Hmm?" Calum glanced up. Brix had ventured further into the room and perched on the coffee table. "Porth Ewan? Where the fuck's that?"

Brix chuckled. "Cornwall, obviously. I reckon you knew that already if your cursing this morning was anything to go by, but if you want the specifics, we're bang between Porth Luck and Rock Down Bay."

Calum had spent his whole life bouncing from Reading to London and back again, but as his rum-addled brain cleared, Porth *Ewan* began to sound familiar. "Is this where you're from? Where your family is?"

"Yup."

"But . . ."

Brix cocked a brow. "But what?"

"Jordan came down here looking for you."

Brix's pale gaze was inscrutable.

Calum winced. "That bad?"

"That's between me and him." Brix's grin returned, but didn't reach his eyes. "I reckon it'll stay that way until one of us dies."

Calum turned that over in his mind. When Brix had disappeared, him and Jordan had been on and off for as long as Calum had known them. He'd assumed they'd broken up, and he'd pondered Brix's fate every day until he'd met Rob, and after that…

After that, he'd become so obsessed with the spell Rob had cast on him, he'd forgotten everyone else.

"Still with me?" Brix touched the sore spot on Calum's cheek and nudged a mug of something hot into his hand. "I've got eggs if you're hungry?"

Calum's stomach growled, but the thought of eating made him heave. "No, thanks. I should call my dad and try and figure a way of getting home. Can I use your phone?"

"Where's yours?"

"In the bin at Paddington Station."

Brix said nothing. Just passed Calum a battered iPhone.

"Passcode is one-eight-three-eight. I'll be outside if you need me."

He stood and returned to the back door, stepping into his wellies before leaving Calum to face the phone alone.

Calum tapped in the passcode and dialled his parents' place in Reading as the acidic notion that Rob might've called there first curdled his stomach. He'd charmed Calum's mum before—the last time they'd come to the city to see him. She'd *liked* him, for all the reasons that weren't fucking true.

I can't do this.

As luck would have it, he didn't have to. The answer machine kicked in, reminding Calum that it was *October*—the time of year when his parents packed their bags and flew to Spain to spend the winter with Calum's aunt.

Shit.

Calum set Brix's phone on the coffee table, ignoring the urge to smash it against the wall. Unlike Brix, his own temper had always been gentle: a slow burn that even friends who knew him well often missed. Not that he had many friends— Rob had seen to that.

And you just let him, didn't you?

Calum got up and moved to the back door. Despite his preoccupation with the end of the world, his gaze zeroed in on Brix, who seemed to be scooping mud out of a wooden box, surrounded by dozens of . . . chickens?

It was probably the most bizarre scene Calum had ever witnessed, but the flock of hens stirred a memory in his tired mind.

"Brix?"

"Yeah?"

"Your van stinks of shit."

"Not just any shit, mate. Chicken shit. Trust me. It's good for the soul."

Calum didn't know about that, but there was no denying the peaceful half smile lighting Brix's face. *He looks happy.* And it was good to see. Despite a wave of envy, Calum was so pleased for him that his chest ached. The Brix he remembered had been a good man, kind and generous with his time. It felt right to see him so content.

Right enough for Calum to brave venturing out of the cosy living room and into Brix's back garden.

He found his shoes by the front door, beside a pair of paint-splattered leather boots he'd recognise anywhere. He stared at them, for a moment transported back in time to his apprenticeship days in Camden, when Brix had been more legend than friend. Back then, those boots had seemed almost mythical, and Calum couldn't count the hours he'd lost to obsessing over the way they hugged Brix's mile-long legs. Legs that Calum was fairly sure had brought his bisexuality to life.

The idea that he might never have fucked men without meeting Brix jarred Calum. He stamped into his shoes and drifted to the back door, gaze once again drawn to Brix, who'd moved on from shovelling mud to scattering straw in a large, fenced-off pen. As tall as Calum, slender, and covered in ink, with his kind eyes and hair long enough to wrap around Calum's fingers . . . yup, Brix Lusmoore was fucking beautiful, even if Calum couldn't imagine being with anyone—bloke or bird—for the rest of his natural life.

"You look like a zombie."

"Huh?" Calum pulled his mind from the gutter to find Brix eyeing him right back, his frown measured, like he had plenty to say but was waiting to see if Calum was coherent enough to hold a conversation. "Oh, nah. I'm all right, just hanging. Sorry you had to see me like that."

"It's okay, mate. Shit happens to all of us. Did you get hold of your ma?"

Calum shook his head. "They're in Spain. The contact details are in my phone."

"The phone that's in a bin at Paddington?"

"Yup."

"Was it an iPhone?"

"No."

"Ah, shame. You can usually find all your stuff again if you get a new iPhone."

Calum ran his hand through his hair, trying to tame it. "Couldn't get a new one anyway. The contract isn't in my name."

"Whose name is it in?"

"My, uh, ex."

Comprehension coloured Brix's features. "Is that what's happened here? You've had a bust up and split?"

"Something like that." Calum turned away from Brix's searching gaze and focused on the nearest thing, which happened to be a near-bald chicken. "What the hell is that?"

"That, my friend, is an ex-battery hen. I think I'm going to call her Ginger."

"Ginger?"

"She might be a red one when she gets her feathers back. Did your ex leave that bruise on your face?"

"No."

"Are you lying?"

"Yeah." Calum glanced around again, noting that Ginger wasn't the only bald chicken scratching around. "Are they all ex-battery?"

Brix's frown deepened, but he returned his attention to the chickens. "Every single one. Started rescuing them a few years back. Got too many now, but, hey, that's life."

"Where do you get them?"

"Factory farms, mostly. They get sent to slaughter when their egg production slows down, but they've got years left in 'em really, if you take care of them right."

"So you rescue them?"

Brix shrugged. "I buy them, actually, the morning their number is up, then sell them on to soft idiots like me."

It was almost too cute for Calum to bear. "What do *you* do with them when they stop laying?"

"Depends." Brix winced. "If they're healthy and happy, I'll keep them going, but if they're not doing so well, I get my dad to, um, you know, so they don't suffer."

Calum got the picture. "Your dad lives close?"

"Close enough." Brix treated Calum to a roguish grin. "He lives with my aunt up at the house."

The house. It rang a bell, and Calum recalled the rumours he'd heard about the dodgy clan Brix came from. He wondered how true they were—if Brix's eldest brother really had killed a man with his bare hands—then he remembered this was real life, not Game of fucking Thrones and shit like that was never true . . . right?

Calum had never had the balls to ask, and though his life had imploded since he'd seen Brix last, that much hadn't changed. He pointed at the baldest chicken crouching in the corner by herself. "What's that one called?"

"She hasn't got a name yet. I was going to take her and a couple of others to my dad, but I cleared some space, so I reckon I'm going to keep all of this morning's leftovers with me."

"This morning?"

"That's where I'd been when I found you at the station. I was on my way home."

"Oh." Calum couldn't think of anything else to say. Embarrassment warred with despair, and despair won out. While Brix had been doing his best for Cornwall's poultry, Calum had been dribbling down his T-shirt on a wet bench.

What a tit.

But a warm bundle of flesh being thrust at his chest distracted him before he could fall down that rabbit hole again. He stared at the bald hen Brix had dropped in his arms. "What the—"

"She's friendly. Think she's gonna be a cuddler."

"A cuddling chicken? That's a thing?"

Brix grinned. "Not often. My lot are bandits. My old man's got a couple he keeps in his pockets, though."

Calum studied the hen in his arms. "She looks oven ready."

"Oi, none of that. She'll hear you."

Brix's expression told Calum he was serious. Calum tempered his amusement and stroked the chicken's head. "You should call her Bongo."

"Bongo? Why?"

Calum shrugged. "Why not?"

Brix stood back and considered the hen. "I s'pose she could be a Bongo. I reckon she's gonna be a good girl. She dropped an egg as soon as she came out of the crate, like she'd been walking in the sun her whole life."

With the hen so warm and soft in his arms, Calum didn't want to consider where she'd come from. "She'll be all right with you looking after her."

"And what about you, eh? You gonna tell me what the fuck's going on?"

"What do you want to know?"

Brix ran a gentle hand over Bongo's placid form. "Anything you need to tell me. I'm not going to force it out of you, but you need to give me something if you're going to stay here."

"Stay here?"

Brix fixed Calum with a look that felt parental. "It don't take a genius to work out you're up shit creek, and I reckon if you had any inclination to hop it home you'd have done it already. Am I right?"

"Maybe." Calum lost himself in Bongo's lizard-like gaze, hiding from Brix's piercing stare. "I guess if I wanted to go home, I wouldn't have wound up here in the first place. It's not like the train didn't stop before I fell asleep."

"So why didn't you get off?"

Calum slowly shook his head. "I didn't want to. I needed to be as far away from him—from there—as possible."

Brix raised his eyebrows, catching Calum's slip. "This is a long way to run. Are you in trouble?"

"What? No. It's nothing like that, I've just . . . lost myself, you know? And I don't know how to get it back."

Brix plucked Bongo from Calum's arms and set her down in the dusty run. "Know how that feels, mate."

Calum didn't doubt it. Brix had always possessed a wisdom that came from a life that had seen too much. "I might get a Wonga loan. It'll get me back to London, at least."

"Is that where you want to be?"

Calum thought of the shop in Rob's name and the barren flat in Paddington that had never felt like home. "I'd rather shoot myself."

"Then stay here, like I said. You don't have to explain yourself. Reckon I know all I need to."

"But I haven't told you anything."

"So?" Brix shrugged, like it was nothing. "I've got a spare room and some guest slots at the studio. It's not like you don't have a trade. You're still tattooing, aren't you?"

Calum snorted. "It's about all I'm doing, but I haven't got any kit. It's—" His voice fell away as his heart wept for Dottie. "Brix, I don't have anything."

Brix laid a hand on Calum's arm, his slender inked fingers wrapping around Calum's wrist like a blanket of heated vines. "Then you best stay right here until we figure this shit out."

Brix threw a tin of tomatoes into the meat sauce on the stove, watching Calum stare a hole through the back door from the couch. Anyone else would've thought him obsessed with the chickens, but Brix knew better. Calum's studied gaze was empty, and whatever he was seeing had taken him somewhere else entirely.

If the subtle distress in his dark eyes was anything to go by, it wasn't any place pleasant, and that was Calum all over —*subtle*—though that was the only thing Brix recognised in the shaken shell of a man he'd once counted among his closest friends.

Not his fault. You're the one who bailed.

The devil on Brix's shoulder also reminded him to nip upstairs and neck his evening meds.

When he came back, Calum hadn't moved.

Fuck this.

Brix got his biggest pot out of the cupboard and clanged it down on the stovetop.

Calum jumped. Brix felt bad for a moment, but the brief spark of life in Calum's tired gaze was a relief. It had been hours since he'd last spoken; he'd clammed up right after agreeing to stay the night in Porth Ewan.

"Sorry," Brix lied. "Checking you're awake."

"I am now."

"Good. You can help me massacre the spaghetti."

Calum looked at Brix like he'd grown four heads, but got up from the couch and drifted to the breakfast bar anyway. "What do you want me to do?"

"Nothin' really. Just fancied some company." Brix filled the pan with water and set it to boil. "And I was shitting it a bit that I'd lost you to the chooks."

"Sorry." Calum scratched his dark beard with a rueful twitch of his lips. "They're kind of absorbing."

Brix had lost more hours watching hen TV than he cared to admit, but he wasn't fooled by Calum's weak grin, and he didn't like it. Calum had always been quiet, but this was something else, and anger tickled Brix's veins.

Some douche bag's chewed him up and spat him out.

"Thought I was the one in a world of my own?"

Brix blinked to find Calum watching *him*, his expression a contradictory mixture of cautious curiosity and apprehension. "What's that?"

"You look pissed off."

"Nah, not me, mate. Just worried I'm gonna fuck up your dinner."

"Doubt it."

"Yeah?" Brix peered at the pan of bubbling meat. "I haven't made this for a while. Might've gone too hard on the garlic."

Bemusement creased Calum's face. "I can't cook for shit. Reckon I've got kebabs and fried rice in my blood."

Brix tried to conceal his displeasure. It hadn't been that long ago he'd lived on his own city diet—cornflakes, and lemon chicken from the all-night Chinese—but his life had evolved since then. Necessity, and the slower pace of Porth Ewan, had changed his ways, and cooking had become an activity he didn't mind too much.

The pasta water came to the boil. He threw in a packet of spaghetti. Calum didn't seem hungry, but Brix was hoping that would change when he had a bowl of food in front of him.

"I'll stir it if you want."

Brix startled. Somehow he'd missed Calum rounding the breakfast bar and peering into the meat pan. "Erm, thanks. I'm a fucker for that. Burnt so many pans I've got shares in Tefal."

Calum raised another weary half smile. "Multitasking, eh?"

"Aye-aye."

"Aye-aye?" Calum's grin widened enough to reassure Brix he was truly with him. "You sound like a pirate."

"In another lifetime, I might've been. My dad and all my uncles live on the sea, my brother did too, on the mackerel tugs and the lifeboats."

"How many do you have?"

"Uncles or brothers?"

"Both, I guess."

Brix swirled the spaghetti. "Three uncles, one brother. Most of them live around here somewhere, except my brother, Abel. He's in Belmarsh."

Calum nodded. "I remember you visiting him. How long does he have left?"

"Two years."

Brix picked up the olive oil, turning away from Calum so he wouldn't have to look him in the eye when he inevitably asked what Abel had gone down for.

But the question never came. Calum reached around Brix

and snagged a strand of spaghetti. He tossed it at the tiled wall. "My nan always told me it was done if it stuck."

Good enough for Brix. He drained the pasta and tipped it in the meat pan. "Grab some bowls, will ya?"

"Okay." Calum glanced around the small kitchen and opened a few cupboards. The second one he tried dumped a stack of tattoo designs on his head.

"Shit, sorry. I keep meaning to collate those."

Calum gathered them up. "What are they? Flash for the studio?"

"Some. Most of them are just doodles, though. Lena, who runs the place for me, puts it all online. I don't have much flash in the studio anymore, unless it's custom—once it's gone, it's gone. I haven't done the same design twice in years."

"Lucky you. I wanted to scrap all the shit I had hanging around my place, but Rob—the, uh, person I worked with— had this idea in his head that the place should look like a scratch parlour."

Brix didn't miss the bitterness. *Rob*. Hmm. He filed it away for future reference. "Where's your place?"

"It's not actually mine."

"*Okay*, where have you been working?" Brix busied himself tossing the spaghetti. "You were destined for big things last I saw, but I ain't heard nothing about you since you left Dark Box."

"Maybe I haven't done anything."

Calum found the bowls and placed two on the counter. Brix served up, careful not to pile Calum's as high as he wanted to. He knew from experience that too much food when you were fucked up made the sick feeling in the pit of your stomach a hundred times worse.

He pushed Calum's bowl along the counter. "If you'd been

doing nothing all this time, I reckon you'd have told me already. What studio were you at?"

"Black Star Ink." Calum accepted the fork Brix held out. "You won't have heard of it, though. I had a long waiting list, but that was probably because there were no other studios nearby."

"Where the hell were you? London's got more studios than I've had hot dinners."

"That's cos you're made of string. The studio was in Paddington."

"Paddington?" Brix let the string jibe slide. "What the fuck's in that craphole that made you settle there?"

"Fuck all . . . that I was interested in, anyway, but the place did okay. I just didn't see much return. My ex handled all the money stuff."

"Rob?"

Calum grunted and studied his bowl of food.

Now we're getting somewhere. Not that forcing Calum to talk when he didn't want to held much appeal, but Brix couldn't deny he was curious. More than that, and had been ever since he'd found Calum huddled on that damn fucking bench. "What kind of work have you been doing? Traditional is still big down here, but we get a bit of abstract and watercolour through the doors, and some of my guys are bang into their neo shit."

Calum's gaze fell on the stag on his hand. "I've done a lot of dot-work sleeves this year, and some geometric stuff. Did a pretty cool portrait a few weeks back."

"Can I see?"

"It's on my phone."

The faint light in Calum's gaze faded like it had never been there at all. Brix touched his arm. "I've got a bunch of pads upstairs. We can sketch after dinner, if you want? I could use fresh eyes on a dagger piece I'm doing for a biker chick."

Calum shrugged absently, and Brix let him be. It wasn't like he didn't know what it was like to be trapped in his own head.

Brix woke early the next day, acutely aware that Calum was on the other side of the wall.

He sat up, listening for any sign of movement from the spare room or downstairs, but there was none, save Dennis yowling on the landing for breakfast.

Brix swung his legs out of bed and padded to the bedroom door, avoiding the creaky floorboard that sounded like another dying cat first thing in the morning. Zelda, came with him, weaving between his legs, doing her best to trip him up.

"Stop it." Brix draped her tiny body over his forearm, a re-creation of a black-and-white photograph Lena had snapped of him last summer when a biker had brought Zelda to the studio door and persuaded Brix that his home was meant to be hers too. Zelda gave him her patented death stare, but her rumbling purr gave her away. Beneath her scathing belliger-ence, she was the sweetest cat in the world.

Brix tickled her chin, then set her down as he came to the spare room. He eased the ajar door further open and took a tentative peek inside. Zelda followed his gaze and sashayed forward, leaping soundlessly onto the bed, sniffing the empty space where, by the rumpled sheets, Brix assumed Calum had been.

Not there now.

Brix went back to his own room and threw a vest over the faded sweats he'd slept in, then he darted downstairs, struck with a stomach-churning fear that Calum had slipped away in the night.

Or worse.

The notion was grim, but Brix couldn't deny the cloud of despair he'd sensed around Calum. Rock bottom was a tough place to be. And if you couldn't see a way out, Porth Ewan offered plenty of scenic places to carve your own.

Numerous nights Brix had considered doing just that flashed into his mind. He stumbled, saving himself on the banister he'd only painted the week before. The smooth satin-wood was cool against his palm, but the blue shade bothered him, like it had since he'd stepped back and studied the finished project. Shame he still couldn't say why.

He bounded off the last step and strode through the open-plan ground floor. Calum was nowhere to be seen, and his shoes were gone from the door. Movement in the garden drew Brix outside, barefoot and shivering against the early-morning chill, and he found Calum by the nearest hen house, holding Bongo to his chest and gazing out at the sea.

"I didn't notice yesterday that you can see the ocean from here," Calum said without turning round. "Didn't notice much of anything."

Brix closed the distance between them and followed Calum's stare. "The seafront is a five-minute walk away. I'll take you there later, if you want?"

"Is it near your studio?"

"They're pretty much one and the same."

Calum nodded and petted Bongo.

"How is she?" Brix asked. "Sometimes the upheaval of being rescued does 'em more harm than good."

"I don't know jack about chickens, but she's doing the same shit she was yesterday. The others seem okay too."

Brix glanced at the bald hens pecking around their run, gobbling up seeds and worms, and looking for all the world like they'd lived like this their whole lives instead of being crammed thirty to a cage and fed on the remains of their siblings. "Bet they've laid too. Never known a battery chook not give me an egg a day. They're good girls."

"I'll take your word for that. I fed your tiny devil cat this morning, by the way. She kept biting my face."

Brix winced. "Er, yeah . . . she does that. Zelda don't mean no harm, though."

"That right?" Calum shot Brix a disbelieving stare before the barest hint of a smile brightened his features. "I didn't mind it, actually. At least you know what you're getting."

The loaded sentence did savage things to Brix's heart. Calum's dark eyes were soulful-deep, and he was in danger of getting lost in them. In Calum's inky hair, chiselled cheekbones, and brawny forearms. And the beard that hadn't been there all those years ago—

Behave yourself, twat. Calum had always been beautiful, but he'd had a girlfriend when they'd first met, and then later, when he'd confessed his bisexuality, Brix had been tied to someone else. Someone who'd left a darker mark on his soul than any ink ever could.

"I used your phone again."

Brix blinked. Calum was staring at him, like he'd spoken already and got no response. "No worries. Who'd you call? Your sister?"

"Fuck no." Calum shook his head. "She's more useless than I am. I called the bank. They gave me an overdraft on an old account that I can live on until I sort myself out. It's gonna cost me a kidney in fees, but it's a lower price than before."

Brix wondered if that meant Calum was staying, and then why he wanted him to so fucking much.

Arsehole. You want his whole life to fall apart?

God, no. But whatever was wrong in Calum's life had already happened. Why else would he be here? And why else would fate have taken Brix past that bench yesterday? Everything happened for a reason. Brix believed that more than anything.

He had to. Or he wouldn't be here to show Calum the way.

CHAPTER
FIVE

Jesus Christ. Calum took in the urban grunge of Blood Rush's inner workings and could hardly believe his eyes. With its black fixtures and fittings, colourful Day of the Dead skulls on the walls, and huge gothic mirrors, the place was about the most awesome studio Calum had ever seen.

He gazed at the sleek leather chairs and the latest-model guns, all interspersed with vintage machines that made his soul weep once more for Dottie. "I like this."

Understatement of the year, but it seemed to please Brix as he shut the shop door. "I work over there. Lee works here. Corey and Kim share the back when Kim's here, which ain't that often these days."

"What's the other one for? Piercing?"

"Fuck no. We don't do that here. If you want your bellend skewered, you'll have to go to the scratcher down the road."

"You sure? I can do piercing for you if there's a demand—"

"Why would I want you to punch holes in people when you can ink?" Brix nodded at the empty bench in the corner. "The spare station is for guest artists. We had Chips Brown in last month. I was going to leave it for a while because I can't be arsed with the hassle of hosting someone else, but I'd love you to do some days . . . if you want to? You can set your own hours and rates. Just pay for the space? Ten per cent?"

It was a ridiculously fair offer. "Twenty."

"That a yes?"

"It's a maybe. What if I don't get any bookings?"

Brix grinned as the back door to the studio opened and an inked woman with electric blue hair let herself in. "*Lena*. This is my mate Calum from London. Can you show him the waiting list? He's worried we won't have any work for him."

By Lena's smile, Calum got the feeling he was about to be shown up. He followed Lena to the reception desk. She powered up the iMac and opened the appointments. "Brix is booked out a year in advance unless he likes a client enough to squeeze them in or he gets a cancellation. Only Corey has slots in the next six weeks. This is the waiting list."

Calum stared. He'd had a waiting list of his own back in Paddington, but nothing like this. "Are they waiting for a particular artist? Or just to come here?"

"Everyone wants Brix, but he only has appointments four days a week. He does drop-ins on Fridays, but only in the off-peak season. It would be mental if he did it over the summer. For guest artists, I offer them up as a drop-in for the first few days, until word gets out and I've publicised them a bit. How long are you around for? I can probably have you booked for the next eight weeks if you're up for it."

Calum shrugged. He hadn't given it much thought, but with a minus balance on his bank account and fuck all else to his name, a month or two of solid work sounded almost too good to be true. "Let's give it a week to start with. I might be the exception to your success."

"I doubt it. Do you have an online portfolio?"

"Nope, but I did the wolf on Brix's neck, if that helps."

"You did?" Lena's expression brightened. "That's my favourite. Brix! Come here."

Brix appeared from nowhere. "You rang?"

"Shirt off."

"Already?" He pulled his long-sleeved T-shirt over his head, revealing his long, slender torso, almost every inch of skin covered in ink, including a large, dot-work wolf that stretched up his spine and curved around his perfect neck.

Calum swallowed. He'd etched the wolf a month after Brix had inked the stag on his hand, but remembered the sensation of Brix's warm skin and the throb of his pulse like it had been yesterday. His low chuckle as he'd no doubt realised the effect his close proximity was having on his rookie protégé. "It's held up well."

"Course it has," Brix said. "It was done by the best."

Calum flushed and looked away as Lena snapped a picture. He'd been proud of the piece, but it hadn't meant much to him for the longest time. Not much had.

"All done." Lena set her tablet down and tossed Brix his shirt. "Now piss off, both of you. I've got work to do."

Lena struck Calum as a woman not to be messed with, so he trailed Brix back to Lee's workstation and studied the ink and stencils that littered the cluttered shelves. "Messy one, eh?"

"The worst," Brix confirmed. "But when you kick out the best watercolour work I've ever seen, I let it slide. Have you seen these?"

He pointed to a series of pictures on the wall. Calum traced one with his finger. He'd seen plenty of watercolour tattoos before, but none quite like the animals and plants in the photographs. He tried to picture the delicate art flowing out of his own gun. Failed, because they looked like they'd been drawn by a fairy rather than inked into flesh. "What's he like?"

"Who?"

"Lee."

"*She's* fucking awesome."

The new voice in the room startled Calum. He spun around to find another woman with neon hair—orange, this time—had joined them, this one complete with lip and septum piercings. "Erm, you're Lee?"

"Yup. What are you and Brix doing messing up my station?"

Beside Calum, Brix chuckled. "Couldn't mess that shit up with a cluster bomb. How do you find anything?"

"Easily, cos it's exactly where I left it if no one arses around with it. Fuck off."

"Watch your mouth," Brix said with a grin that told Calum he and Lee talked this way all the time. "I was just showing Calum your stuff."

Lee eyed Calum before she zeroed in on the stag on his hand. "Oooh, so you're the one with the famous stag? Brix told us about you."

"He did?"

"About your hand," Brix said. "I've got the stencil on the wall. Look."

Calum followed his gaze to Brix's station and saw that Brix had indeed kept the inky stencil from so long ago, framed it, and nailed it to the wall. "Jesus, it's been years since I last saw that."

"How many?"

Calum glanced at Lee. "Too many."

"I'd say so," Brix said.

Lee whistled. "You two are old."

"He is," Calum said. "I was always the young pretender."

"You weren't pretending at anything that I recall." Brix folded his arms across his chest. "Smashed every job from the get-go."

Heat burned Calum's chest. He turned away from Brix's piercing gaze and Lee's obvious curiosity and pointed to the first watercolour piece on Lee's slice of the wall. "How did you get the ink to drip like that on the skin? The last one I did came out too pale."

"You're diluting the ink too much. It took me a while to get it right, and I only do watercolours. It woulda taken me years if I was doing all that macho black-and-grey shit too."

"Hey," Brix interjected.

Lee grinned. "It's so easy to wind you up."

"Nice."

"I think so." Lee returned her focus to Calum. "He loves me really."

"Yeah, like a mallet to the nuts."

Lee ignored Brix's grumble and pointed at the ink detail Calum had drawn her attention to. "I can show you a few tricks if you want? I've got time this morning. I only came in early to order some greens I need for the ferns I'm inking next week."

Calum glanced at Brix, who shrugged and pushed himself off the counter he'd been leaning against. "Fill your boots. I'll get your station set up and you can have a play around. I'm sure someone's got some spare skin you can test the waters with."

"You can do my foot," Lena called out. "I've got a gap needs filling."

Despite the dark mood still plaguing Calum, the urge to set a needle to skin made his palms tingle. "What do you want?"

"No fucking idea. I'll harass you later."

Lena turned back to her work as Brix knocked Calum's arm with his fist. "I'm gonna leave you to it for a while. Gotta nip home, then track down my old man. Just let Lena know when you're ready to take walk-ins. Or not. Do whatever you want. It's all cool."

He walked away before Calum could answer, striding through the studio and out of the front door. Calum watched him go, missing him already. Being with Brix had been the only thing stopping him losing his mind, and as the studio door swished shut, anxiety clawed at his heart.

What the fuck am I doing here?

It was lunchtime before Brix made it back to Blood Rush. He appeared at the station he'd assigned to Calum with a weary grin that broke Calum's concentration.

Calum withdrew his borrowed gun from the young woman's skin and mopped up some stray blood. "All right?"

Brix nodded. "Aye-aye. You?"

Calum ignored the infinitesimal rush that came with Brix's gentle Cornish accent. "Am now I've got a gun in my hand."

"Figured as much. Art is cathartic, eh?"

"That's what Lee said."

"Smart girl."

"Yeah? She said you taught her that."

Brix hummed and ventured closer, peering over Calum's shoulder at the peacock feather he was etching on the woman's hip. "Nice."

"Will be when I've finished."

"I'll bet." Brix turned his gaze to the woman. "How are you doing down there? Not too painful is it?"

The woman shook her head. "Not as bad as I thought it'd be."

"That's cos Calum here's got the softest touch in the business. You picked a good day to walk in here. Tell your friends."

He left Calum to it and drifted to his own station. Calum felt his attention drawn to Brix, but the buzz of the gun was stronger than his fast-growing reattachment to his old friend, and it wasn't long before he lost himself in his work, not looking up until the feather was complete.

"All done." He shut off the gun and pushed his stool back. "You want to check it out?"

The woman staggered to her feet like most people did when they'd been under the needle a couple of hours. Calum steadied her, then guided her to one of the huge gothic mirrors in the studio, bracing himself for the torturous wait to see if the woman liked what he'd done. He hadn't had many negative reactions, but the way his luck had gone recently—

"Oh my God. I love it."

Calum let out a breath. "Yeah?"

"Fuck yeah." The woman turned her body from side to side, viewing the tattoo from every angle. "The detail is amazing. Is the eye made of dots?"

"Yeah, with some white ink. Dot work is my specialty, so I find it really hard not to sneak it in somewhere."

"I love it. Thank you so much."

"No worries. Come back to me when you're ready and I'll wrap you up for your journey home."

The woman nodded, still entranced by her ink. Calum let her be and returned to his station to clean up.

Lena waited for him. "I think I've got one of your clients coming in tomorrow."

"What?"

"I just heard you say that dot work is your specialty, and Brix told me you had a studio in Paddington."

"So?" Calum turned his back on Lena and started dismantling his borrowed tattoo gun for cleaning.

"This guy was booked in for a dot work leopard at a studio in London. Said he'd waited months to get in with the best dot work artist in the city, only to find out that the studio had closed down overnight."

Calum's stomach did an uneasy flip. "Why are you telling me this?"

"Because I want to know if we've got the best dot work artist in London on our books. No other reason, Calum, I swear. No one here will give a shit about the rest of it. The fact that you're Brix's friend is enough."

"Cheers."

"Cheers? That's all you have to say?"

"What do you want me to say?"

"Are you CJ Hardy or not?"

"I'm *Calum* Hardy." Calum didn't turn around, but Lena appeared on the other side of the chair, her gaze almost as piercing as Brix's.

Almost.

Calum sucked in a breath. "Whatever. I worked at the studio. But I didn't own it. Whatever's happened since I left is nothing to do with me."

"Fair enough. Do you want your client back?"

"No."

"All right. I'll leave him with Brix and give you the afternoon off. That okay?"

"It's fine."

"Good." Lena started to move away, but seemed to think better of it. "Fair warning, I don't keep secrets from Brix. So if there's anything about this he doesn't know, you should tell him today."

Sunday marked the fifth morning in a row Brix had woken to find Calum already up and outside with the chickens.

"You're going to turn Bongo into a lap hen."

"That a bad thing?" Calum didn't look up from the chicken dozing in his arms. "She butted my leg until I picked her up."

Brix's chest warmed, and the early-morning breeze faded away. "I've had a few like that. Mary Killigrew was my last one."

"Mary what?"

"Killigrew. Long story. Starts with ancient pirates and ends with my aunt Peg."

Calum shook his head a little. "I feel like I just met you."

The comment seemed out of context, but Brix got it. He'd spent far too much of the past few days searching for the cheerful dude he'd used to know, but the change in Calum was as dark and moody as his beard.

His hot as fuck beard.

"I had a chat with Lena last night," Brix said.

"Yeah?" Calum set Bongo down as his shoulders tightened. "She tell you I'm a fly-by-night tea leaf or some shit?"

"No, she said leopard man from the other day was one of your clients from London. Didn't say much else, but I knew your place had closed down because she told me when the client booked in."

Brix left out the blanks the client had filled—the boarded-up doors and trashed interior. He couldn't work out what Calum's old studio had meant to him, but he didn't fancy telling him that anything he'd left in the place had been swiped or destroyed.

Unless he already knows.

Lena hadn't seemed to think he did. *"He looked shocked, Brix, and freaked out. That bloke's gotta story, I'm telling you."*

Brix couldn't disagree, but most folk who worked at Blood Rush had a past they didn't want to talk about. Why would Calum be any different?

"What do you want me to say?" Calum folded tense arms across his chest. "I already told you—and Lena—that the shop wasn't mine."

Brix didn't like Calum's defensive stance. It didn't suit him. "I don't want you to say anything. I'm just letting you know you can, if you want to. I ain't gonna judge you if you're in trouble. Lord knows, I've had my fair share of shit-storms coming from my clan."

"Clan?" Calum tilted his head to one side. "I heard on the street yesterday that you come from a family of gangsters."

Brix snorted. *"On the street*? In Porth Ewan? Yeah, okay."

Calum looked as convinced as Brix felt every time Calum deflected his questions. "I haven't seen much of the place except ink and chickens."

"Easily fixed. Lena and Kim are coming over later, but I can show you around a bit this morning if you like?"

"You mean the beach?"

"And the rest. Get that shitty new coat of yours and I'll show you the magic."

"Shitty?"

"Yeah, *shitty*. That bundle you picked up at the charity shop looks good on you, but it ain't gonna keep you warm if you're still around come winter. The wind is vicious here. My ma used to say it carried the demons ashore."

"Even yours?"

Brix zipped up his own coat. "Especially mine."

Brix hauled himself up the rocks, climbing a path he knew like the back of his hand. The sea had eroded some of the ancient formations he remembered from childhood, but this route to the highest cliff in Porth Ewan Bay never seemed to change.

He reached the halfway ledge and glanced over his shoulder. Calum was a heartbeat behind him, dark gaze more alive than Brix had seen so far, leading Brix to wonder why he hadn't brought him out sooner. "All right down there?"

"Fuck yeah. Keep going. I want to see what it's like from the top."

"Just a sec." Brix veered off the steep path and rounded a crumbly verge. The opening to the small cave couldn't be seen, but he knew where it was. Had done since he was knee-high to a grasshopper.

He crawled inside, feeling around for any sign that Peg had moved the counterfeit DVDs here after they'd disappeared from his garden. His hand hit a thick plastic sheeting. The type Peg's crew used to protect their goods when contrary bastards like Brix forced them to stash their shit in the vast Lusmoore cave network hidden amongst the cliffs. What lay beneath the sheeting felt like DVDs, though the few packages he felt could only hold half the amount Peg had dumped in his backyard.

Good. They're moving them on. Brix never knew what drove him to check up on the family business he'd worked so hard to distance himself from, but it was something he found himself doing time and time again. Reassurance, maybe? The DVDs pissed him off, but he'd found far worse over the years.

"Brix? You in there?"

Brix withdrew his hands from the contraband. He'd forgotten Calum waiting outside on the windy cliffs. He backed away from the loot and shuffled out of the cave, barging straight into Calum, who wasn't where he'd left him.

Calum steadied Brix with gentle hands. His light touch burned, quickening Brix's pulse. Or maybe it was the sea air going to his head. It had been a few weeks since he'd made this climb. Yeah. That was it. It had to be, because there was no way the surprise in Calum's eyes was mirroring the shock in Brix's heart.

After a protracted moment, Brix regained his footing. Calum released him and shot him a quizzical frown. "What were you doing in there?"

"Just checking something."

"Something?"

"Plenty of shit I don't want to talk about either. Fair's fair, ain't it?"

Calum scowled, though there was no anger in his gaze. "You got me there. I'll keep my gob shut. I'm assuming you don't want anyone to know you go crawling around the caves up here?"

"You assume right, but I'm not worried about you running your mouth. You barely speak to anyone."

"I don't know anyone."

"You know me."

Calum's halfhearted glare mellowed to the crooked grin Brix had dreamed about in years gone by, the lopsided smile that made his eyes gleam. "I talk to you."

Brix grunted and pushed ahead of him on the cliff path. "Do you bollocks. You talk to Lee more than you do me."

"Jealous?"

"What do you think?"

Brix toasted a grin over his shoulder, but the spark in Calum's gaze faded. "I was just messing, man. Didn't mean nothing by it."

He looked down at the hiking boots Brix had lent him, apparently lost in the art of putting one foot in front of the other.

Brix frowned. *Did I miss something?* He had no idea, but if the past few days had taught him anything about this new, subdued version of Calum, it was that these loaded silences needed to be filled, or else hours could pass before Calum spoke again. Besides, was it really his business that Calum and Lee had hit it off like *they* were the long-lost mates?

Maybe you are jealous. And the masochist in Brix couldn't let it go. "Has Lee been showing you her tricks?"

"Hmm?"

"Lee."

Calum caught up. "She's shown me loads."

"Good." Brix pulled himself through a narrow gap in the rocks. "That's how we roll at Blood Rush. Share the love, you know? I want everyone to grow as an artist, not worry and bitch over who's making the most dosh."

Calum followed Brix through the rocks. "Where I came from, I couldn't leave a sketchbook lying around without someone ripping my designs and selling them on."

"That's cos you've been surrounded by cunts."

Brix regretted his crass bluntness as soon as the words were out, but Calum shrugged.

"You're probably right. In fact, you *are* right. Maybe that's why I've found it so hard to draw these last few years. Remember when we used to get a crate in, and some JD, and a bunch of us would draw all night, collaborating the fuck out of everything we did? I miss that."

"Then you've come to the best place. We have sketch nights all the time. Don't plan 'em, they just happen."

"Sounds good to me." Calum drew level with Brix and peered over the edge of the path. "That's a long way down."

"Give it a minute."

Brix grabbed Calum's arm and pulled him up the last few steps of the path and out onto the cliff that had been the top of the world for as long as he could remember. "My dad brought me up here when I was born and dangled me over the edge, presented me to the sea. Tradition for Lusmoore babies. And the Carters who have the caves across the bay, but they're land people really."

"Always knew there was legend in you somewhere." Calum kept his gaze on the view—the grey sky, the misty clouds. The crashing waves below, and the miles and miles of moody-blue ocean. It was like nothing else on earth, and Brix wondered if Calum could feel the Cornish magic Brix had been born with. The fabled histories that were still sung by the fishermen who hung around the Sea Bell in town, and the Joker in Porth Luck.

"Don't be daft, boy. Emmets aren't like us. You'll see when you go on chasing your dreams to that big city you're always blathering on about."

Brix caught up with Calum as he drifted to the edge of the

cliff to study the deadly rocks below. "Ever told you why they call me Brix?"

"Nope." Calum didn't look away from the crashing waves. "It's always screwed with me, though. I know you did your apprenticeship in Brixton, but Jordan told me you were Brix way before that."

Brix found a grin, forcing back the bad taste in his mouth that just a mention of Jordan's name brought. "My dad called me Brix. He took me to London once, and Brixton was the only name on the Tube map I could read. I wanted to go there, but he dragged me to the dogs in Walthamstow instead, grumpy old git. Reckon he thought the name would wind me up, but I loved it, and now . . . it's who I am."

"Who were you before?"

"Benjamin. Did I never tell you that either?"

Calum shook his head. "It makes sense now, though. You could be a Benjamin."

"Not in this lifetime." Brix shuddered. "Learning to write was a whole lot easier once I'd lost a few letters."

"Eh? How old were you when you went to London with your dad?"

"Too old not to be able to read the whole map or write my own name. I was twelve before I had those down."

"It doesn't show."

Brix snorted. "Why do you think I went into business with Lena? I couldn't do what she does on my own. Can barely make sense of the booking system, let alone everything else."

"You're not stupid, Brix."

"Oh, I know that; least, I do these days. Just had a different start to most emmets. Different kind of education, I guess."

"What the hell is an emmet?"

Brix retrieved his hip flask from his inside pocket and took a swig before passing it Calum's way. "An outsider . . . a non-Cornish person. Some Porth Ewan folk believe none of you should be let over the border."

"What do you think?"

"I reckon the world would be a darker place without the souls that keep us warm."

Calum shivered and swigged from the flask. "You must need a lot of them to stay warm around here."

Brix let the turbulent sea reclaim his gaze. "You'd be surprised. You can come up here wanting to jump and go home a few hours later with a new skin. This place is magic, and it's in my blood. Without it . . . well, who knows where I'd be."

CHAPTER
SEVEN

Calum paced the spare bedroom in Brix's cosy cottage. Voices and laughter filtered up from the kitchen, but despite Brix's open invitation, he felt no urge to join them. In fact, the thought of traipsing downstairs and presenting himself to Brix's mates—even though he knew Lena already—made him want to throw himself out of the nearest window.

Imagining it took him back to the cliff-top adventure Brix had taken him on that morning.

You can come up here wanting to jump . . .

Brix had uttered the words like they meant nothing, but the flash of pain in his eyes had struck Calum like a lightning bolt. He'd stepped closer, his arms outstretched, silently asking Brix to lean on him and set free whatever shadows had brought him home to Porth Ewan, but Brix hadn't seen him move. He'd closed his eyes to the wind and turned away, signalling that it was time to go home.

Home.

Calum swallowed a bitter laugh. He hadn't known where that was for a long time. Brix had taken the soul from London when he'd left all those years ago, and Reading held nothing for him except the poky house he'd grown up in. No lifelong friends or treasured memories. No ties, no bonds. Which left him hiding in Brix's spare room, jumping out of his skin every time a burst of laughter reached his ears.

Idiot.

He made grand plans to skulk in his room all afternoon, but Brix woke him up sometime later. "Hungry?"

Calum rubbed his eyes. "What?"

"Hungry. It's five o'clock."

Damn. It had been barely three the last time Calum had looked at the retro alarm clock on the bedside table. He sat up, helped upright by Brix's strong hands. "Did your friends go?"

"No." Brix eyed Calum steadily. "That doesn't mean you can't come downstairs and have some dinner, does it? Can't stay up here forever."

The miserable bastard in Calum wanted to do exactly that, but the gnawing hunger in his belly betrayed him . . . along with a need to escape the scorching heat of Brix's touch before he embarrassed himself. "What's cooking?"

"Paella."

"Paella?" That got Calum's attention, and explained the smoky scent of paprika and garlic wafting through his open bedroom door. "Didn't fancy a roast?"

Brix smirked. "Oh, I did, but Kim and Lena had other ideas."

Lena. Calum had dodged her since she'd dropped her bomb about the fate of Black Star Ink. And he'd taken her advice to be elsewhere when his abandoned client had come in to see Brix.

Cal, you're such a pussy.

"What are you thinking so hard about? Don't like fish?"

Calum returned to reality. Brix had leaned closer while

he'd been gone—too close if he'd been anyone else—so their faces were inches apart. "What are you talking about fish for?"

Brix stared for a heavy moment before he blinked and pulled back. "I wondered if you didn't like it. There's chicken in the paella if you don't, and chorizo. You can pick out the squid."

Calum nodded, finally understanding. "I like fish. Just not sure I'm in the mood for company."

"It's not company. It's Lena and Kim. You know Lena, and Kim wants to meet you."

"Can't I meet her at work?"

"Just come down. Have some food, say hello. Ten minutes, then I'll leave you in peace, I promise."

Brix slugged Calum's arm and left the room.

Calum dragged himself off the bed and peered in the nearby mirror at his wayward hair. Rob liked it neat, but since Calum had invaded Brix's life—a man who'd never sniffed a hair-styling product in his life—he'd let it grow and succumb to the wild Porth Ewan wind, leaving it a shaggy mess of dark curls. Not his best look. Or was it? He'd always felt like a twat with a head of hair wax.

You're still a twat now.

Calum found some socks and went downstairs. In the kitchen, he expected to find another woman with fluorescent locks to add to Brix's collection. Instead he found Lena talking the ear off a scruffy dude who made Brix seem tidy and big. Calum had been caught out again, as Kim, it seemed, was a bloke.

A friendly bloke, if his wide grin and outstretched hand were anything to go by. "All right?"

Calum shook Kim's hand, forcing a smile. Meeting Rob's

mates had never panned out. Apparently, Calum wasn't good with people.

Can't you handle a bit of adult conversation?

Well sure, if adult conversation didn't mean shouting over each other about how much money they had.

"Cal?" Brix was staring like it wasn't the first time he'd called Calum's name. "You want a drink?"

Probably a bad idea, but something made Calum nod anyway, and Brix pressed a bottle of cold beer into his hand, pushing him gently towards the kitchen table. "Park yourself. I'll get the grub."

The grub turned out to be a huge shallow pan of chubby yellow rice laden with chicken, seafood, and spicy sausage. With all the bickering going on around him, Calum couldn't work out who'd cooked it, but it was *good*. He was on his third helping when he caught Brix watching him.

Calum shoved a prawn in his mouth and raised an eyebrow. Brix mirrored the gesture, his eyes twinkling with an emotion Calum couldn't decipher. So he looked away, turning his attention to Kim, who was arguing with Lena in a language Calum had never heard.

Brix came to his rescue. "Stop yabbering in Cornish. Cal ain't got a clue what you're on about."

"Sorry," Kim said. "It's habit when she gets on my dick about leaving tools all over the bedroom."

"Bedroom?" Calum glanced between Kim and Lena, noting for the first time how their bodies were angled towards each other, their shoulders touching. "Sorry, I hadn't clicked you're together."

"*Together*." Lena poked Kim's ribs. "That's an interesting concept for the only mug who'll put up with you."

Kim swatted her away. "Like you're a picnic."

"Compared to you?"

"Easy," Brix intervened. "Sunday supper club ain't for your bitching."

"True enough." Kim shovelled the last of his food into his mouth and pushed his bowl away. "Calum, I saw the mandala you did yesterday. That's some awesome shit. Surprised we haven't heard of you."

Calum glanced at Lena, who stared steadily back. "No reason for you to have heard of me. I'm not that good."

"Yes, you are." Lena rapped her knuckle on the table. "I put your work on the website last night, and you've got appointments every day this week. If you want them, of course. I didn't take deposits, just in case."

"In case what?"

"In case you didn't want to work every day for the next week. You're self-employed. You can do what you want."

What I want? If only Calum knew what that was. If only he'd ever known. "I'll do them. Got nothing else on, have I?"

"Except chicken whispering," Brix said. "Pretty sure I caught you singing to Bongo yesterday."

Calum broke his stare-off with Lena. "Oh yeah?"

"Wouldn't be the first time you've serenaded a bird."

"If you're referring to Stacey from Bethnal Green, you can fuck off."

"Oooh, sounds juicy," Lena said. "Do tell."

Brix shook his head. "Nah, I'm a gentleman, but if you've never heard a drunk Reading lad sing Valerie from the bottom of an East End high-rise, you're missing out."

Calum laughed, couldn't help it, though his humour was heavy, weighed down by the knowledge that the Calum who'd the balls to do stuff like that was long gone. "I blame that scrumpy you made us all drink. Fucking stuff was like acid.

I'd have tried flying if my legs coulda carried me to the top of those flats."

Kim grinned. "Brix, you should get 'im over your old man's place. Give him some home brew."

"No, thanks." Calum drained his beer. "That hangover still haunts me."

Brix got up and started clearing the table. The cats howled for their dinner at his feet, and he opened a cupboard and cursed. "Fuck. I didn't bring their food from the shed when I got back from the wholesalers. Give us a hand, Kim?"

Calum pictured the giant sack of dry cat food Brix had brought home the previous evening. He'd wondered where it had gone. Things seemed to disappear in Brix's house and garden, like the stack of crates that had been here the first day he'd come. They'd evaporated overnight, leaving Calum to consider the possibility that they might've been a figment of his drunken imagination.

Kim and Brix went outside, which left Calum with Lena. Dodging her keen gaze, he gathered the last of the dishes and took them to the sink, hoping she wouldn't follow.

She appeared at his elbow a moment later. "You wash. I'll dry and put away. Don't suppose you know where anything goes yet."

"Okay."

"Are you going to sulk forever?"

"Sulk?" Calum rinsed a plate and passed it over. "What are you talking about?"

"I'm talking about the fact that you've hardly spoken to me since Wednesday."

Calum couldn't deny it. "Sorry."

"No, you're not."

He couldn't deny that either.

Lena sighed. "Look, I know you're pissed with me for telling Brix about your old place, but I had to. He wouldn't like it if he found out and I hadn't told him. I wasn't stirring, I promise. I haven't told him any of the shit your ex has written about you online."

Calum dropped a jug into the sink, splashing them both with water. "What?"

"The weaselly guy with the glasses and bad quiff? Apparently, you stripped his shop, punched him when he tried to stop you, then ran off with all the money."

It would've been funny if it weren't so tragic. Calum shook his head. "That's not what happened."

"I know. You turned up here with a black eye and no socks, and I can tell by the way you moon at Brix that you wouldn't hurt a fly."

Calum didn't know whether to be offended or embarrassed. "I don't moon at Brix."

"Okay. Like he doesn't moon right back."

Calum opened his mouth. Shut it again.

Lena laughed. "Dude, quit catching flies. It's okay. Your secrets—all of them—are safe with me. I only told Brix about your old place because I had to. The rest of it's none of my business."

Calum was saved from having to answer by Brix and Kim coming back. He drained the water from the sink and took the tub Brix had filled with cat food to the corner of the kitchen where Zelda and Dennis had their bowls.

Dennis sprang onto the counter with surprising grace. Zelda climbed up Calum's back and punched him in the face.

Amazing. Perhaps Porth Ewan wasn't such a safe place after all.

Lena and Kim left not long later. Brix walked them out while Calum fended off attention from Zelda and lost.

She'd settled in by the time Brix returned.

He laughed. "She'll have the shirt off your back next."

Calum didn't fancy admitting that Zelda already slept on the small pile of not-new clothes he'd bought at the charity shop. "She's all right."

"No, she ain't. She's an arsehole. Always has been. I just love her anyways. She's a bit like Lena, really. You two make up while I was outside?"

"We never fell out."

"Liar."

"Am I?" Calum plucked Zelda from his shoulder, ignoring her grumble. His conversation with Lena had settled the disquiet he'd carried since she'd confronted him on Wednesday, but the way Brix was looking at him now made him want to hide behind Dennis's impressive bulk. What was it about this bloke that made it feel like he was staring into Calum's soul?

Fucking Brix and his blue eyes.

But for once, Brix didn't seem oblivious to the effect he was having on Calum. "All right, enough of the angst for one day. I reckon we could do with more beer. Fancy a pint and a shanty sing-along?"

"A what?"

Brix grinned. "It'll make sense when we get there. I need to catch up with my old man, and I reckon you could do with getting out of the house."

"I've already been out of the house. You dragged me up a cliff, remember? And the studio."

"Doesn't mean you can't come out again. Besides, you love the studio."

True, though Calum was still getting used to the pirate-punk music. "You don't really want me to sing, do you?"

"No. I want you to come out for a pint. It's no fun on my own."

Brix smiled and every mechanism to refuse him withered and died.

Calum darted upstairs with Zelda hot on his heels and peeled off the T-shirt he'd napped in, searching out a clean one. A noise behind him sounded like Dennis. He turned, expecting to see the giant cat digging through his socks. Instead he found Brix in the doorway, eyes wide, clutching a stack of his own T-shirts.

"Fuck." Calum wrapped his arms around his bare torso, wishing the floor would swallow him up.

Brix averted his gaze. "Thought you might need to borrow some stuff. Er . . . sorry, I'll leave these here."

He dumped the T-shirts on the bed and disappeared. Calum shivered and let his arms drop, already back in London, clutching a soggy bag of chips outside Rob's favourite cocktail bar.

Sure you wanna eat them?

Fuck's sake. Embarrassment—*frustration*—tossed Calum's gut. It had been a long time since he'd been half naked around Brix, longer than Calum cared to remember. Or perhaps he did care to remember, and that was the problem, because even without the ink, *Brix's* body was a work of art. Limbs for days and sinewy muscles. Not that shit like that mattered. In the rare moments of peace Calum had ever had from Rob's games, it hadn't been Brix's *body* he'd imagined. No. It had been his eyes . . . and his voice. Damn. Brix had the best voice.

Zelda appeared from nowhere, springing onto the bed and

making a beeline for Brix's T-shirts. Calum rescued them, pulling his own shirt on, and took them across the landing.

Remembering Brix of old, he expected to find a scene of chaos—piles of clothes, sketchbooks, and art supplies. Instead, he found a bedroom so neat and tidy it was almost sterile. The only thing out of place was a washbag on the bedside table that looked like it belonged in the bathroom of someone else's house, and a shiver slunk down Calum's spine.

Get out of his room.

Fucking hell.

Calum fled and found Brix with the chickens, turning over the earth in the runs. He leaned on the fence and watched, his new favourite pastime. Who knew chickens fighting over worms could be so entertaining? Not that Bongo got any; she was too placid to fight—or too lazy. Calum hadn't decided. He stopped Brix as he passed with the spade and snagged her a worm. Then he bent over the fence and scooped her up, dangling it into her beak.

"Jesus Christ," Brix muttered.

"What?"

"You're gonna be the death of me."

Brix flung his spade down and stomped into the shed, leaving Calum with the chickens and the worms.

Calum stared after Brix, watching through the tiny window as he shifted sacks of animal feed around with more force than seemed necessary, and his stomach churned again. The idea that he'd somehow annoyed Brix made him feel sick.

Actually, it scared the shit out of him, and his head began to spin, anxiety crushing his chest.

Maybe Brix had read whatever Rob had written about Calum on the internet. Maybe Lena had lied and shown him anyway, or he'd found it of his own accord. Trashing people online was one of Rob's favourite things to do.

Fuck them, Cal.

Swallowing bile, Calum recalled every hateful post he'd ever seen Rob write—Twitter, Instagram…and his head spun harder, cold sweat beading his skin.

"Hey." Brix waved a hand in front of Calum's face. "You look like someone just killed your dog."

"I don't have a dog."

"Your pops not got that golden retriever anymore?"

"Hettie?" Calum pictured the time his parents had visited him in Camden with his father's hearing dog. "She died years ago. My dad's got a Labrador now, a black one, I think. Barney."

"You think?"

Calum shrugged. "I haven't seen them in a while, and my parents don't do technology."

He didn't add that Rob binned any post that wasn't his. What was the point? Whatever had driven Brix into the shed seemed to have faded, and Calum wanted to keep it that way.

"Pub, then?" Brix said.

Calum nodded and ducked back inside to grab a wallet empty of anything except a basic debit card, trying not to think about what that meant, hanging onto the fact that having fuck all money was weirdly liberating.

It's not liberating. You're fucking broke.

The unavoidable truth sent Calum's pulse to his ears again. If he could pull regular sittings at Blood Rush for a while, he could make the payments on his loans and give Brix rent, but what would happen when his time was up? Even if he found a studio to take him, where would he live? *How* would he live without Brix?

"Shittin' hell, mate. You coming or not?"

Calum jumped.

Brix was right there, and Calum dug deep for a smile.

"Sorry. Away with the fairies."

"Are you fuck. Fairies are fun. You can tell me what's really bothering you on the way."

On the way turned out to be a windy walk inland to the Sea Bell, a dilapidated pub that was packed with ruddy-faced local men, clutching jugs of ale and shouting along with the band of fishermen holding court by the front bar.

"Shanty Boys," Brix shouted over the booming folk song.

"All the clans up this coast have a lad or two that sing. It's local lore."

"It's what?"

"Lusmoores, Bosankos. Penroses and the rest. We're primordial residents. Been here as long as the ocean. Hear that?"

Calum listened to the sea hymn being sung by men who looked no more like choir singers than Brix did a primary school teacher. The song was *loud*, and reminded Calum of the music Brix played at Blood Rush, without the heavy metal and bagpipes. "I like it."

"Good. Cos you'll hear a lot of it round these parts. What you drinking?"

"Whatever you're having."

Brix nodded and said something to the barmaid. Two mugs of amber ale appeared a moment later. "From the brewery up the road in Rock Down.

Calum took an experimental sip, and then another, deeper swallow. "I like that too."

"Course you do. I remember you drinking Guinness by the bucketload. Always knew there was an ale-swiller in you somewhere."

"What else did you know?"

Brix leaned closer, their bodies already wedged together by the crowded bar. "That one way or another, you'd be in my life forever."

Someone shouted Brix's name, saving Calum from drowning in Brix's electric gaze.

Pulse pounding, he downed more beer, seeking solace in his pint glass until something warm bumped his leg.

He glanced down to meet the warm gaze of a border collie. The dog was attached to a bright-red lead. Calum followed it, expecting to see a burly fisherman, but instead, he found himself face-to-face with Lee, the last person he'd expected to see in a pub like this. Though, to be fair, with her Doc Martens and grungy green beanie, she didn't look out of place.

Calum scratched the dog's ears and grinned at Lee. "Who's your friend?"

"Rocky. I stole him from my sister for the day."

"Why?"

"She's a cunt."

"Hey." Brix leaned around Calum and socked Lee's arm. "She's trying, remember?"

"Yeah, trying to be annoying."

"You're pretty annoying yourself. Give peace a chance, gal."

"Dick." Lee scowled and turned away. Calum wondered if she might storm off as abruptly as she'd arrived. Calum had grown used to the edgy banter between Brix and Lee, but this seemed different, like she'd meant her muttered insult. But Brix's answering silence spoke a thousand words, and after a protracted moment, she turned back and offered Brix a sheepish grin.

"Sorry."

"Don't worry about it. But you can make up for it by looking after Calum while I go find my dad."

"I don't need looking after." Calum knocked back half his ale. "I'm fine on my own."

"I know," Brix said. "It's Lee needs watching. Last time she was in here, she throat-punched my uncle."

Lee's glare returned. "Did not."

"Did so. Just stay with Calum and behave yourself."

Brix pulled Lee's hat over her face and walked away, shouldering through the cramped bar until he disappeared entirely.

Calum looked back at Lee and raised an eyebrow. "Why did you punch Brix's uncle?"

"Because he's a lecherous prick. Don't be fooled by Brix. He's the best bloke in the world, but the rest of his family are wankers."

It wasn't the first time Calum had heard whispers of Brix's family being trouble "Are they that bad? Really?"

Lee rolled her eyes. "Don't give me that boys will be boys shite. Brix's uncle isn't some dozy old man who doesn't know how to talk to women. That's the *point*. He didn't see me as a woman. He called me a little poof cos I'm the only trans person he's ever met in his life."

"Oh." Calum stared at Lee, taking in her elfin features and youthful skin, all marred by a defensive belligerence that told him she was waiting for him to say something totally fucking stupid. "Erm . . . Well, maybe he's a bigger cunt than your sister then."

A pause stretched out.

Then Lee laughed. "Yeah, okay. You might be right about that. Still think you should buy me a drink, though."

Whipped, Calum bought more beer, a handful of vodkas for Lee, and a couple of whiskeys with the last scrapings of cash in his account. "Find me somewhere we can talk."

Lee clipped Rocky's lead to her studded belt and relieved Calum's tray of a few glasses. Then she led him around the bar to a quiet-ish corner he hadn't seen. She dumped the drinks on a sticky table, then dropped into a tatty leather armchair, tucking her feet beneath her.

Watching her, Calum necked a whiskey and then pulled a stool to the table, before pinching one of Lee's vodkas. "I didn't know you were trans. I'm fucking sorry if I've put my foot in my mouth these past few days."

Lee tilted her head. "You haven't. Why would you think that?"

Calum shrugged, no sensible answer coming to him, and his silence drew Lee forward.

"You're not always wrong, you know."

"I'll take your word for that."

"I suppose that'll do until you learn to take your own."

Calum drank more beer.

Lee laughed. "You're so cute."

More beer.

"Damn." Lee shook her head. "I really am bad at being nice. Are you more comfortable when I'm an arsehole to you? Or are you just more used to it?"

Calum's glass was empty. He set it down, searching for words. Finding them. Discarding them and starting over, while Lee relaxed, as if the everlasting wait for someone to connect their brain to their voice box was normal to her.

Eventually, the truth came to him. "It's me, not you. I'm not used to being around good people. I don't know what to do with myself when you say nice things to me."

"Sounds like someone else was the problem then. Not *you*." Lee scratched Rocky's ears. "But I get it. Before I came here, I had one amazing friend, but he's kinda wild, so I was pretty feral when Brix took me in."

They'd made a considerable dent in their drinks. Calum got up and nodded towards the bar. "Hold that thought."

"Only if you let me pay."

Calum took Lee's debit card and loaded up again. Back at the table, he let curiosity win. "Tell me how you met Brix?"

Lee claimed her vodka and kicked back in her seat. "The friend I was telling you about...he disappeared for a while. When he came back, I'd left home and wound up down here, sleeping on the beach at Fistral Bay. He knew Brix could help me, so he brought me to him, and I'm still fucking here."

"Did he give you a cuppa and bed for the night too?"

"Me and everyone else." Lee smiled into her drink. "He collects us like his hens. Life support we don't know we need until we wake up one day and realise we're still breathing. He gave Lena half the shop, you know…when her and Kim were about to go under. Stopped Kim from offing himself, I swear."

"Lena and Kim are definitely together, then? I get mixed messages from them."

"They're bonded, I guess, but they both have other people too. They live on that commune out near the farms. Into all that free love and stuff."

That explained the vibe Calum hadn't deciphered between Kim and Lena. "What about Corey? Brix save him too?"

"Yup, from whatever weird shit he was up to before he came to Blood Rush. Brix saved us all, and I'm glad of it. Means no one looks at me like I'm a skank."

"So that's why none of you looked at me that way either. Used to it, eh?"

Lee shrugged. "We're used to Brix taking care of people. I've never seen him with anyone like you, though."

"Like me?"

"Like he *is* with you," Lee clarified. "He's so chill when you're in the same room. That Lusmoore edge fades, you know?"

Calum hadn't been around Brix enough the past few years to judge. He filed Lee's observations away and pressed her a little more. "How did you end up this far south? You don't sound Cornish."

"Derby," Lee confirmed. "Dead-end village near the Peak District. Got run out of town when I told my dad I wanted to transition. It was the last straw for him after I'd been outed as the village gay."

Calum snorted. "Bet you weren't the only one."

"Yeah, but it was obvious with me. I was never exactly masculine, you know? I might as well have worn a sandwich board and rung a fucking bell. I couldn't believe how shocked my parents were when I told them. I'd lived with it so long in my head, it didn't feel weird anymore."

"How old were you then?"

"When they found out I was into lads?"

"Yeah."

"Fourteen. I got caught watching gay porn online and my dad beat the shit out of me and convinced himself it was a phase, and I never admitted to being gay, which made it easier for him to push it under the carpet. I like girls too, though, and everything else."

"Me too." Calum gulped ale to disperse the lump in his throat. "What happened next?"

"Nothing for a year or so, then all the gender stuff started fucking with my head. So I told a teacher at school and they forced me to tell my parents."

Grim dread took hold in Calum's gut. He knew where Lee's tale was going.

"My dad threw me out on the spot." She pulled a face of forced nonchalance. "Said I'd done it on purpose to embarrass him. I sat on a table outside the post office all day, thinking he'd calm down, but then the village idiots came after me with bats and pipes. He'd paid them fifty quid to chase me to the coach station the next town over."

"Jesus." Calum blew out a breath. "How long ago was this?"

"A few years. It took me a month to wash up down here in

my sister's neck of the woods, though. I tried London first, but it wasn't for me—just like Saint always said."

"Saint?"

"My friend. You'd like him, if he ever stayed still long enough to meet anyone new. He's as clever as Brix."

Calum believed Lee's friend was as amazing as she said he was, but it was hard to imagine there was anyone in the world quite like Brix. *I love him.* As a mate, obviously.

Obviously.

Reading his mind, Lee downed the last of her vodka and picked up Calum's pint. "Brix is a good boss *and* a good mate, by the way, in case you were worried about how working for him is going to affect your friendship. He cooked me dinner every night when I had my boobs done."

"No, I *brought* you dinner every night. Never said I'd cooked it all." Brix appeared at Lee's shoulder and eyed the detritus of the drinks Calum and Lee had put away. "Seems like I've got some catching up to do. Your sister's here, though. Want me to take her Rocky?"

"Nah, I'll do it."

Lee and Brix disappeared, Brix to the bar, and Lee to the car park to deliver Rocky, the world's quietest dog, to her sister.

Brix returned first, laden with enough whiskey and vodka to make Calum's eyes water. "Lee been telling you her life story?"

"About a saint and a white knight." Calum belatedly realised how drunk he was. "You're the white knight by the way."

Brix scoffed. "Hardly. She's just never understood how far her friends will go to protect her."

"What does that mean?"

Brix drained one of the whiskey glasses. "Put it this way,

you wouldn't want to be one of the idiots up north who beat her with a pipe."

"You…?"

"No." Brix shook his head. "I gave her a *tattoo* gun. But the other bloke she's talking about is the most dangerous fucker I've ever met. And I've met some dangerous fuckers."

Lee came back as Calum absorbed that, her trademark scowl firmly in place. "Are we ditching this shithole, or what?"

Brix necked another whiskey. "To go where? The Slug and Lettuce? No fucking chance. I'm too old for that, luv. So is Cal."

"Not as old as you." Calum shot Brix a hazy glance. "Definitely too drunk, though. I need a kebab."

Brix laughed. "In Porth Ewan? On a Sunday? Dude, you can't even buy a bag of sugar after nine o'clock."

Calum frowned. "I don't want any sugar. Where's the bog?"

Brix pointed over his shoulder with his thumb. "By the dartboard."

"Ta." Calum hiccupped and stood. The warm rush of too much booze swept over him, but instead of the black shame of the rum on the train, this buzz was good—*really* good—and the long-neglected devil in him wanted to drink a hell of a lot more.

He found the gents' and relieved himself, staring in the cracked mirror as he washed his hands. His eyes were bloodshot from a bellyful of ale and whiskey, but for the first time in days he felt human.

Lucky me.

Calum returned to the table to find Lee getting ready to leave.

"She's off to the chav hole," Brix explained. "Wants to drink bubble-gum vodka and listen to bad house music."

"Nice." Calum tried to hide his distaste, but failed as Lee rolled her eyes and punched his arm.

"I'm going to meet my missus, thanks very much. You're just jealous, both of you, cos you ain't getting any."

Brix looked away, gathering their empty glasses into a neat stack. Calum shrugged. He hadn't had sex in months, which made sense now he knew for sure that Rob had been getting fucked elsewhere.

Cos you weren't man enough to do it, remember?

The lull in Calum's bad mood evaporated. He reached for his drink and downed it, feeling the warm ale gurgle into his stomach. Suddenly, stumbling back to Brix's cottage and passing out in his borrowed bed seemed like the best idea he'd had all night. Preferably without ever waking up.

Sensing the shift, Brix stood and pulled Lee's hat sideways. "Who are you meeting? Just Vicky?"

Lee righted her hat. "And her brother. We're going home together. Don't go all mother hen on me now. You've had all night."

Brix made a face and pulled the hat off entirely, stuffing it in his pocket. "Whatever. I'll walk you to the dirt hole, then I better get Mr Pisshead home."

"Hey." Calum rose, but coherent thought abandoned him as he shrugged into his coat, and the moment passed.

They took their glasses to the bar and left the pub, stepping outside into the cold night. Calum shivered, feeling it more than he had up on the cliffs. "Where are we going?"

"Home," Brix said. "With a quick detour on the way. That cool?"

"Yeah, I'm cool."

Brix chuckled. "Yes, you are. Coolest motherfucker I've ever known. You're the only one don't know that shit."

Calum took a breath.

Brix tapped a finger to his lips. "Shh. Come on."

They set off in the direction of the seafront, Lee between them, though she was definitely the least drunk.

"You got hollow legs?" Calum wove around a drain cover. "I'm pissed as shit over here."

"It's the air," Brix murmured, sageness lacing his deep voice. "You'll always get arseholed quicker by the sea if you're not used to it."

Lee laughed. "What's your excuse then? You're as twatted as him."

"I'm not used to *drinking*. I'm a good boy, remember?"

"Old git, more like." Lee poked his side. "You should see him and Kim, Calum. They look like hooligans, but they'd rather make jam with the old ladies than come out with the rest of us."

That wasn't the Brix that Calum remembered, but he knew there were better ways of having fun than pissing it up every night. "I like jam."

"Good," Brix said. "And you, squirt . . . watch your lip. You know Kim don't drink, and you know why. Everyone's got their shit. They don't need you mouthing off about it."

"Yeah, yeah." Lee stuck her tongue out, less offended by Brix's reprimanding than she'd been in the pub, and they reached the seafront without incident.

Lee hugged Brix. "I'll text you when I'm home."

"You'd better. No scrapping, yeah?"

"Yes, Dad."

Lee pulled back with a smirk and skipped inside.

Calum watched her melt into the crowd. "Think she'll be okay?"

"I reckon so." Brix's hand brushed Calum's elbow as he guided him back the way they'd come. "I heard a rumour that friend of hers is back down south. He'll take care of her, even if she doesn't know it."

Calum was too drunk to dissect that. So he went with the obvious. "Doesn't seem to stop you worrying, eh?"

Brix turned his gaze to the distant sea. "Not much does when you're as old as me."

"You're thirty-three."

"So? My granddad didn't make fifty."

"Don't mean you won't make a hundred. Is this why you don't drink much? Cos it makes you morbid?"

"Hmm? What? Oh, yeah, sometimes. Just can't handle my beer." Brix grinned, but it fell flat. Calum held his gaze for a long moment, until Brix shivered against the cold wind. "Come on. I need my bed."

They drifted back to the cottage. Brix let them in and tossed his keys on the side. "There's a spare set in the drawer by the fridge. Take them so you can get in when I'm not about."

"Why? You going somewhere?"

"Not often, but you don't want to be stuck with me all the time, do you?"

Or perhaps Brix didn't want to be stuck with him.

Jesus, Cal. You're as interesting as my nan's couch sometimes.

"Thanks."

"No worries." Brix yanked his boots off. "Actually, now I think about it. I won't be around tomorrow for a while. Will you be okay going to the studio on your own?"

"I'm not in till two."

Brix laughed. "Ah, that's right. You have Rubi?"

"That's what it says in the diary, next to a note that says *viking shit* and no contact details, so I have no fucking clue what I'm doing."

"It'll work out."

"What if it doesn't?"

"Trust me, it will. You're gonna have the chillest afternoon ever."

Calum believed Brix for no other reason than he was *Brix*. "Where are you going tomorrow? Anywhere nice?"

"Nope."

Okay. Calum considered the pensive frown that had cinched Brix's brows. "Is it bad that I feel like another drink?"

Brix raised his gaze from the floor. "You'll think so in the morning, but there's some of my dad's scrumpy around here somewhere if you're brave."

"Scrumpy? Is it worse than what you gave me in London?"

"Definitely. Can't remember a thing if I have too much of it."

"Sounds like my kind of drink."

"Does it?" Brix opened the door to the cellar and ducked inside, reappearing a moment later with a plastic container of what looked like piss. "What do you want to forget?"

"Nothing specific."

"Ah." Brix nodded like Calum's nonanswer made sense. "Wanna forget *who* you are for a while, eh? I get that."

"Doubt it," Calum said. "Seems to me that you've got everything in place down here. Ink, mates, family. The perfect life."

"Nothing's ever perfect. All that shit you just said . . . it's a perception. You can't count on anything 'cept yourself, and even that's a bonehead idea." Brix opened a cupboard, retrieving glasses that were smaller than Calum expected for cider drinking. "Now sit the fuck down. You'll want to be on the couch for this."

Calum followed Brix to the living room and sat on the sofa. Brix claimed the other end and opened the scrumpy.

"Me and Abel used to call this Scrumpty-Dumpty when we were kids. I drew a drunken egg as a logo, and we sold it at the bottom of our drive every summer. My dad let us keep half the money."

Calum leaned forward and accepted a tumbler of amber cider. "Who sells it now?"

"No one. Abel's banged up, remember? And my dad doesn't make so much these days. Too busy spending all his dosh on the horses."

"You've never told me why Abel went to prison."

"I know." Brix took a long, slow swallow of cider. "I never told anyone back in London, cos it felt like if I kept quiet, it wouldn't be real, even though Abel was closer to me there than he is now. Stupid, eh?"

"Not really. You can be right next to someone and worlds apart."

"True that. I guess it depends how deep you bury your soul, and how deep the person beside you is prepared to go looking. What do you make of the scrumpy?"

Calum took Brix's abrupt subject change at face value and let Abel Lusmoore go. He reached for the cider and took a drink. Instant fire burned down his throat and set his insides alight. "Fucking hell."

Brix laughed, his dark frown all but gone. "My nan used to say it was like swallowing sunbeams, but my dad didn't make it as strong back then. These days, he sets a batch to brew, then forgets all about it till the barrel's about to blow."

Calum believed it. He took another swig, absorbing the

roiling heat. It reminded him of another heady burn, one he hadn't felt for—

"Jesus. It's got you already."

"What?" Calum opened his eyes to find Brix watching him, *amused*. "I'm okay."

"Oh, I know you are. I remember the look on your face right now. Means you're gonna fall asleep smiling."

"You think? I haven't done much of that lately."

"You'd be surprised. I reckon you smile most when you don't know you're doing it."

Calum sat back, prepared to take Brix's word for it, but Brix jumped up with more grace than Calum could ever hope to have and went to the cabinet by the window. He pulled out a battered photo album Calum hadn't seen in years and brought it to the couch.

"Proof," he said by way of explanation, his words heavy and slurred, like his own skinful had caught up with him. "Let's find us happy."

Curious, Calum forced himself upright and scooted along the couch. In his drunken stupor, he overshot and bumped into Brix, who didn't appear to notice, or feel the jolt of electricity where their knees touched.

Damn.

Must be the scrumpy.

Fuck it.

Calum took another deep swallow. "Show me the happy."

Brix gulped more scrumpy and opened the album, flipping forward a few pages until he came to what Calum recognised as Brix's converted warehouse flat in Camden, the scene of *many* rowdy parties. Calum couldn't count the long summer nights he'd spent on the balcony, talking, drinking, smoking, all to the soundtrack of whatever music Brix had been in the mood for back then.

"Makes me want a spliff," he murmured—a whisper, really.

Brix sighed. "Me too, but I gave up the smokes, and the weed. Gotta be clean, believe it or not."

Calum reached for his drink, trying to ignore the irony, and keep the question out of his eyes as he gazed at Brix for a deepening moment.

Failed, as Brix shrugged and drained his glass. "Living hard caught up with me. Can we leave it at that?"

"Sure, but . . ." *Is that why you left?*

His voice fell away before the words became real, and Brix slid the album into his lap. "That was your missus, wasn't it? Can't remember her name."

"Lucy." Calum glanced at the photo absently, his mind lingering on the mystery of Brix.

"Have you had any girlfriends since her?"

"Hmm?"

"Since Lucy. I remember you banging a few blokes, but I always figured you'd end up with a bird. You seemed more comfortable with them."

"Not really." Calum turned a few pages until he came to a photo of Brix sitting on a bench outside the Camden studio, his clothes grungy and dark, hair held back with a gothic bandana. "I'd just never met a bloke who wanted to do more than fuck."

Brix poured more scrumpy. "They're hard to find."

"What about Jordan? I thought you two would go the distance."

"I don't want to talk about Jordan."

Oops. Calum's inebriation had obscured the warning lights

flashing around Jordan. Did Brix know what had become of him? Last Calum heard, Jordan had moved to Amsterdam.

He turned another page. Brix moved closer to peer over his shoulder. Warmth where they touched seared through Calum, eclipsing even the scrumpy-induced burn in his gut. "I'm—er —still looking for the happy."

"It's there. Keep going."

They were about ten pages in when Brix let out a low hoot. "And there it is. Happy Calum, grinning away to himself like no one's watching. Game, set, and match to me."

Calum stared at the photo of himself, circa 2009, all dodgy jeans and faded band T-shirts, his hair cropped short in an ill-advised buzz cut. "What a tool."

"Aw, don't be a dick. You're happy. Look."

Calum looked again and couldn't deny it. He had no recol-lection of the night the photo had been taken, but his carefree smile was so genuine it seemed to belong to someone else. "Did you take this?"

Brix shrugged. "Maybe. I always had that old Nikon knocking around that flat, and you were my favourite subject."

"Was I?"

Brix's grin turned sheepish, and he flipped forward a few more pages, all of them crammed with image after image of Calum smiling to himself, clearly off his nut, or staring into space like a gormless idiot.

Calum didn't get it. "Why me?"

Brix set the photo album aside and grasped Calum's shoul-ders, his gaze sliding into an intensity that made Calum's head spin. "Because I wanted to show you something you'd never see on your own. Mate, you're fucking beautiful. Has no one ever told you that?"

The urge to be flippant was strong, but Brix's eyes held

Calum hostage, rendering him mute, and leaving him devoid of anything except a silent head shake.

Brix leaned closer and pressed their foreheads together, his lips just a hairsbreadth away. "Well, they should've, cos you are—"

Calum's mouth found Brix's in a soft, cider-flavoured kiss, a brush of lips that took him by surprise as much as it seemed to Brix, whose hands flew to Calum's face, though he didn't pull back. Their lips met again, the kiss growing in intensity with a subtle burn that stole Calum's breath, prickled his skin, and quickened his pulse to a stuttering, *familiar* rhythm.

Shit.

Memory descended on Calum like a bird hitting a window. *That night—*

The kiss faltered and Brix drew back, eyes wide, derailing Calum's jarring recollection of a hazy night too many years ago to count. "I . . uh. Fuck."

"Yeah," Calum breathed. "I don't know how that happened."

"Same as it did last time, I'd imagine."

Calum's heart skipped a beat. "You remember that?"

"Course I do. I fell over my own feet outside Koko's. You caught me, and I threw myself at you to say thanks. I think...?"

Brix's grimace was so comical that the heady tension between them eased a little, memories fading again. The drunken kiss they'd shared on that damp Camden evening had been seared on Calum's soul until he'd met Rob. Now, even with his lips still burning from *this* kiss, it didn't feel real.

Calum brought a hand to his head, trying to catch his breath. His thoughts. *Anything* to make sense of this moment. "I was so hammered that night I nearly dropped you."

"Fun, though, wasn't it?" Brix's frown morphed into a rueful grin. "I thought about it a lot after."

"Me too. It was a crazy night."

Brix hummed, then seemed to notice his hands still gripping Calum's face. He let them drop, leaving Calum mourning the loss of his touch, craving the rush of warm palms against his skin. "I'm fucking wankered."

The abrupt shift stung before Calum realised Brix's sentiment was mutual. "Either that, or your walls are moving."

"You've got the scrumpy spins." Brix got up and meandered to the kitchen. He returned with a bottle of water. "Drink this before you go to sleep. Have a banana when you wake up. You'll puke otherwise."

He flopped back on the couch, throwing an arm over his eyes. Calum waited for him to resurface, but it didn't happen. Brix's breathing evened out and his arm slackened, slipping off his face, to reveal that he had, in fact, passed out cold.

Calum was mesmerised—Brix was as enchanting in sleep as he was awake—but his own need to lie down caught up with him fast. He considered sliding to the floor and letting the scrumpy mould his bones to the hardwood boards. But waking up on the shop floor in Paddington on the *many* nights Rob had gone walkabout with his keys, still made his back ache.

Fuck that.

He got up, found a blanket, and covered Brix with it, reality slowly filtering through the swirling cider haze, along with a festering urge to kiss Brix again.

Don't.

He settled for tracing a fingertip over the ink on Brix's forearm and squeezing his hand. "Thanks for everything."

Gentle bites to Brix's cheek brought him awake. He raised a heavy hand to bat the biter away, but a low, grumbling hiss warned him off, and he knew better than to declare war on that.

On *her.*

Brix opened his eyes to the bundle of feline attitude digging the shit out of his chest.

Zelda stared back at him. Belligerent. *Awake.* She wanted him up, but why? Despite the beginnings of a searing hangover already settled in his bones, it was too dark to be morning. Even Porth Ewan wasn't this black at dawn.

And this isn't my fucking bed, either.

The thought solidified as Zelda leapt from Brix's chest to the back of the couch, revealing he'd never made it upstairs.

Fuck. Brix winced and sat up, holding his throbbing head as he took in the scattered detritus of a night on the scrumpy. *Jesus. Whose bonehead idea was that?* As if he didn't know it had been his—cos it was always his now Kim had got his shit together.

Reeling, Brix staggered to his feet, using the sofa for

balance. Zelda's reasons for waking him were her own, but the fact remained that it was twat o'clock in the morning and he was downstairs in his clothes—even his boots—which meant he had shit to do before he could go back to sleep.

He stumbled upstairs, for once not pausing to see if Calum was in his bed, and went straight to his bedside table and the washbag of distant guilt and self-loathing that kept him alive. The fat red pill stuck in his throat, but he forced it down, kicked off his boots, and collapsed on his bed, before Mother Nature had other ideas.

Too slow.

Sudden nausea ripped through him, dragging him off the bed. He dashed for the bathroom and puked in the sink.

Fuck, fuck, fuck. There was no way the pill had survived that.

So take another one.

He didn't want to, but life wasn't about choices anymore. Not for him. It was about necessity. Survival. Which meant sleep was off the table until that fucking pill stayed down.

It was light when he woke again, tucked up in bed, his boots on the floor beside him, and no delinquent cats to be seen. Brix rubbed his eyes, wondering if he was truly awake, but the blaring alarm from his phone a split second later put paid to the idea that it was all a dream.

He scrabbled around, searching for the phone.

The one in his jeans…that he was still wearing.

Twat.

Brix silenced the alarm, noting the time: 8:30 a.m.

Fuck's sake.

He was due in Truro at ten, the place that always seemed to be dragging him from his bed when he felt like utter shite.

Spinning, he hauled himself upright. Nausea followed him, then a blinding headache, and a dull pain in his stomach that would be his constant companion for the rest of the week, and it was only Monday.

Couldn't just have a couple of beers, could you?

Apparently not. Brix reached for the washbag before it slipped his mind. He swallowed the two gigantic pills—one red, one blue—and stumbled to the bathroom, searching out water to chase them down. And to brush his teeth while he avoided the red-eyed, unshaven corpse staring back at him from the mirror. It was definitely a bandana day, if he survived that long.

Shower.

The hot water woke him up enough to remember Calum, and that for the short time they'd lived together, Brix had yet to get up in the morning before him.

Today was no different. But where was he? Out with the chickens?

Brix backed away from Calum's door and glanced out of the landing window. The yard was empty, the house quiet, and there was a distinct lack of feline activity too.

Bemusement, and the need to eat something before he hit the road, drove Brix downstairs.

The cats were on the couch, sleeping in and around a blanket from the armchair. Apart from telling him they'd been fed, the scene stirred something in Brix—the couch, the blanket...scrumpy, Calum, and...*fuck.*

Brix gripped the banister, the events between the pub and waking up in his bed, impacting like a runaway freight train. The confusion in Calum's dark eyes as he'd looked at pictures of himself. The bewilderment when Brix had told him why there were so many.

The sensation of Calum's skin against Brix's palms, and his lips . . . fuck, his lips.

Christ.

Dizzy, Brix gripped the banister harder, digging his fingers into the blue wood. In the cold light of the early morning, he couldn't recall how Calum had responded to their clumsy kiss, if he'd let Brix feel the warmth of his broad chest as they'd fallen against each other, or if he'd humoured him then let him pass out like the drunken idiot he was.

Everything was hazy and shadowed, and all he truly knew was that the cats had been fed, but Calum was gone.

"You look pale. That winter flu caught up with you already?"

"Hmm?" Brix turned away from the window as nurse Sally stuck a needle in his arm, drawing blood. "Nah, I'm hungover. Went out last night."

Sally twisted the cap onto the vial and dropped it in a plastic envelope. "That's not like you. Given up clean living?"

"No, just felt like a blowout. And now I wish I was dead."

"Most people do after a heavy night. Don't be so hard on yourself."

"Howdya know I'm being hard on myself?"

"Because I know you, mister, and you always are."

She was right on both counts. Sally had been his key nurse for the last four years, and she was as familiar with Brix's bouts of self-loathing as he was.

"I shouldn't drink. It fucks my medication up."

"As far as I remember, it only interferes with your treatment when you drink your dad's scrumpy. Ben, there's nothing wrong with having a few pints with your friends."

Ben. Brix rolled his eyes. Sally was the only person on earth who called him that. For some reason, he'd never told her anyone he'd met more than once called him Brix—*no, it's cos you want to disassociate this shit from your real life.* "It was the scrumpy," he admitted. "I usually give it away when my dad brings it round, but I have a . . . friend staying with me at the moment, and introducing him to it seemed like a good idea at the time."

"A friend, eh?" Sally's faint smirk let Brix know she hadn't missed his stumble. "How's he this morning?"

"Dunno. He was gone when I woke up."

Misery hit Brix again, laced with an unhealthy dose of nausea.

Sally passed him some water and let it drop. "How are you otherwise? Your bloods were good last time, as always, so you must be doing something right."

"I do what I'm told." Brix found a distant grin and plastered it on his face. "I'm okay, though. Got some new chickens and my dad's behaving himself. Can't ask for more than that."

"No fights in the Sea Bell?"

Brix's grin became genuine as he recalled his father's last rumble in the pub. "It wasn't a real fight. Just a fisherman thing, scrapping over the hurling ball."

Sally was from Birmingham, and it showed when Brix talked about Cornish things like they were anything close to normal. "Remind me what that is again?"

"The ball they throw from the sea wall on Shrove Tuesday. A mob game for fishermen, cos whoever has the ball when the clock strikes noon gets free beer for a year at the Sea Bell and the Joker. That shit's important to my dad."

"Do you play?"

"Fuck no. I'm not Cornish enough for that."

Sally frowned. "Not Cornish enough? You were born here."

"But I left, and some folk round here say that makes me as good as dead."

It was lunchtime when Brix finally slipped through the studio's backdoor, hoping to reach the office before anyone saw him. But luck wasn't on his side and he found Lena already there, frowning at the appointment book she used to back up the computer system that remained a mystery to Brix. "Can't you do that somewhere else?"

She glanced up. "What crawled up your arse?"

"Nothing."

"You're not as hungover as Calum, then?"

"Calum?"

Lena set the book aside and studied him over the reading glasses that made her look like a punky secretary. "He was pretty ropy when he dropped by this morning. Did you have a good night?"

"No idea. Woke up on the couch at 3 a.m."

"That bad, eh? Speak of the devil . . . Hey, Calum."

Brix jerked around faster than his aching head could deal with. Calum stood in the doorway, dishevelled and gorgeous . . . too fucking gorgeous if he felt even a fraction as terrible as Brix did.

"All right?" Calum sidestepped Lena, who flipped Brix a wink and *left*. "Did you get your shit done?"

"Shit?"

"You said you had stuff to do this morning." Calum

frowned, shyness creeping into his dark gaze. "Did I imagine that?"

Brix couldn't handle the uncertainty in Calum's pretty eyes. The *dejection*. "I'm impressed you can remember anything I said yesterday. I can't and I need some fucking tea."

More than tea. Dizziness hit him again and he regretted not getting round to forcing breakfast down before he'd left the house.

"Brix?"

"Yeah?"

Warm hands gripped Brix's wrists. "Sit down, mate."

I'm not sitting already? Apparently not. Calum guided Brix to the chair Lena had vacated and crouched in front of him, those warm hands on Brix's knees. "You okay?"

Brix nodded, slowly, knowing his head would spin off his shoulders if he moved too fast. "I need to eat. Is Corey here? He's usually my pal when I'm hanging. Kid's fucking awesome at fetching butties from Becky's."

"Becky's?"

"The sandwich place." Lena reappeared at Calum's shoulder. "What do you want? I'll get it."

"Anything." Brix drew the appointment book towards him, hoping Calum would go with her and give him the space he needed to get himself together.

Calum didn't leave. He kept his hands on Brix's knees. "What's wrong?"

"Hangover."

"And?"

And so many years when Brix had longed for Calum's earnest gaze to keep him company through the worst days of his life. But he couldn't get into that right now. He'd break, and he wasn't in the mood to be fixed. "*And*, I'll be fine when

I've eaten, honest. Are you telling me you didn't wake up with a hole in your head this morning?"

Calum's shy grin made a rare appearance. "I *woke up* at the top of the stairs. Didn't have a fucking clue what had gone on. I'm all right now, though. Kim brought me some bacon."

"He's good like that." Brix forced himself to contemplate how much *didn't have a fucking clue what had gone on* covered. And also, how he'd stepped over Calum to reach his own room. "Did you tuck me up in bed?"

"Erm . . ."

"Don't answer that."

Calum rose and perched on the desk instead. "I didn't want you to get cold."

No chance of that with Calum around. His presence was flustering Brix with every day that passed, and it was gradually dawning on him that it had always been like this. That Calum had bewitched him from the start.

"Brix?"

"Yeah?"

"What appointments do you have today?"

Brix had no idea. He focused on the handwritten book Lena kept up-to-date for his sake. "A consultation and finishing up a half sleeve."

"You want me to stay with you? I've got a while before that viking dude comes in—"

"I'm fine." Brix scrubbed his eyes and tried to unfuck his face. "Do what you gotta do. I'll be out in a bit."

A week actually passed before the viking appointment made it to the studio. By then, Calum had been staying with Brix for a fortnight that passed Brix by in a flash. *It's like he's always been here.* And if he didn't think about the elephant in the room their drunken night had become, it had been the easiest two weeks of his life.

And he didn't think about it…much.

Yeah yeah.

Calum's appointment arrived at 10 a.m on Monday morning, the studio empty aside from Brix, Calum, and Lena.

Brix met him at the door. "Here comes trouble."

"Brixicles." Rubi Matherson wrapped his big arms around Brix, an embrace from an old friend that moved mountains. "How've you been, brother?"

Brix choked into a laugh."Same old, same old. You know it's not Kim you're booked in with, right?"

Rubi released Brix from his bear hug. "He okay?"

"Aye-aye. Just busy with other things."

"Other things, eh?" Rubi had been a Blood Rush client for as long as the studio had been open, and he had a nose for gossip. His gaze slid to Lena. "That be you? Or are you too busy teaching my BFF how to use that angsty wangdoodle of his?"

She middle-fingered him. "Don't start."

Rubi blew her a kiss. "Wouldn't dare. One raging Khaleesi is enough for me."

"Good boy. Have a biscuit."

Lena tossed Rubi a fairing cookie. It kept him quiet until his keen gaze landed on Calum. Then interest flared in his hazel eyes and he propped a big shoulder on the wall. "You here for me?"

Calum had his nose in a sketchbook. "Think so. Damn…" His dark gaze found Rubi's skin. "You sure you have room for more *viking shit*?"

Rubi laughed, the sound filling the room. "Honestly, I don't care what you do or where you do it. I come here for the peace and quiet."

It made sense to Brix, but not to Calum. A frown creased his face, and despite the complex world Rubi came from, he wasn't the type to leave someone hanging. "It's like this: I either come here for a kip, or you can cart me off to Harvest House."

Harvest House. Brix's heart bottomed out, a split second blip that tuned him out of Calum questioning the name, and Rubi's response.

"…where they send you when you're proper tapped out."

A bitter laugh escaped Brix before he could stop it. "There's worse places than that."

Calum swivelled his attention to Brix, but Brix was done. He needed out, and he backed away, the scent of disinfectant thick in his throat. The clang of keys loud in his ears. *Fucking hell*. Why did some memories fade while others stuck around forever?

He left Rubi with Calum and retreated to his own station. The half-finished sketch he needed to be ready by lunchtime. A dozen other things he'd let slide.

Rectifying it took his full focus. Or maybe he made it like that, cos he *needed* it. Either way, the next time he glanced up, Calum was absorbed in some skin on Rubi's left hip, and Rubi was...asleep. Of course. Which was probably as well. Calum didn't talk much when he worked, his gaze intense, tongue caught between his teeth. Gorgeous enough that there was no way on earth Rubi wouldn't have noticed.

So what if he notices? Rubi's single and Calum isn't yours.

And Brix couldn't deny that Rubi was hot. Tall. Big. Clever. All the things Brix wasn't.

You are tall, bozo.

Brix flicked a glare at the back of Lena's head. *Get out of my brain.*

Lena obliged, which left Brix at the mercy of his thoughts and his terminal curiosity. Calum's specialty was dot work, but Rubi was already covered in nordic ink etched in Kim's signature style. Matching them would be tough, but this was Calum. If anyone knew how to blend in it was him.

Leave them alone. If anything, to let Rubi sleep. His life was a murder of chaos—literally these last few years. *Let him rest.*

Brix found something else to do. And then he ran out of time to obsess over Calum's broad shoulders and his bearded jaw. His own client arrived and kept him busy for the rest of the day. Rubi was long gone by the time he took a breather, and Calum was MIA too.

At least, it felt that way until Brix found him in the break room, engrossed in something on the iPad Brix didn't know how to use either.

"Watcha doing?"

Calum jumped. "Fuck. Oh, it's you."

"Expecting someone else?"

"Not on purpose."

"Eh?"

Calum sighed. "I'm trying to get a new phone, but my credit score's worse than I thought."

"Why?"

"Lots of reasons."

"Share on. It might help."

Calum got up and went to the sink to rinse mugs that weren't his. "I borrowed a lot of money a few years ago. I got behind with the repayments pretty much straightaway and I haven't done much to repair the damage since."

"And your old phone was in your ex's name..." Brix remembered that. And it made sense. Inactivity on a bad credit file was almost as bad as fucking up in the first place. "Which means you've been invisible for a while, eh?"

Calum nodded, his gaze still in the sink. "The bank only gave me an overdraft on my old cash account because I've had it since I was thirteen."

"I didn't know banks existed when I was thirteen. I was too busy popping wood over the hot fishermen." A truth more than a joke. "What are you going to do?"

"Nothing. I don't need a fucking phone. Who would I call?"

"Me. And whoever you called with the phone you had before."

Calum laughed, but the brittle sound held no humour, and Brix knew he was missing something obvious. Then he recalled his own spell in the wilderness when he'd returned to Porth Ewan. How his phone had found its way to the bottom of the cliffs, and it had been weeks before he'd seen fit to replace it.

"What about a SIM-only deal? I've got an old iPhone at home you could borrow, and paying the bill might help your credit score."

"You've done enough for me. I can't borrow anything else from you."

"Buy it from me, then. I was gonna sell it to Corey for fifty quid."

"Fifty quid? For an iPhone? Piss off, mate."

"You think I'd lie to you?"

Crickets.

"Seriously?" Brix rocked back on his heels. "It's a phone. And I'm not a fucking liar."

"I know, it's just—"

"Just what?"

A long pause stretched out before Calum finally turned around. "I'm sorry, okay?" He stuck his hand in his back pocket and pulled out a few notes. "I'm not used to anyone who's not my mother giving a shit about me."

"I give a shit."

"I *know*, and I'm sorry I'm being a twat about it."

Brix wanted to ask if being a twat about it included neither of them mentioning that kiss.

But he didn't. He took Calum's money and left him to it.

An hour passed before Calum came to find him. "I ordered a SIM."

"Good stuff." Brix kept his eyes on the stencil he was prepping for the following day—a polka-trash pinup girl with far more colour than he'd ever used when he'd first started tattooing.

"Lena said I need to show you the photos of Rubi's piece before she deletes them."

"Okay." Brix set his work aside. *How the hell does she know I haven't seen it already?* "Let's have it."

Calum held out the studio's iPad. "I didn't get a before shot."

"That's okay." Brix took the tablet. "We don't post Rubi online, or any of his mates who come in here." Calum didn't ask why, but Brix felt the need to fill the silence. "They're from the Rebel Kings Motorcycle Club in Whitness, which means as long as you work here, you can't tat anyone from another club."

"What other clubs?"

"Dog Crows, mainly. But I wouldn't ink them anyway."

"You don't like them?"

"They're nothing like Rubi." Brix swiped the iPad screen, scrolling through Corey and Kim's recent work until he landed on a tattoo that seemed to jump out of the screen. "Wow. You fucking nailed that."

Calum leaned closer. "You think so? He said he wanted a lark flying over a river, but there wasn't a lot of room."

"You made room." Brix traced the flawless dot work water that flowed seamlessly into Rubi's existing tats. "You've created a snapshot in time, and he'll appreciate that forever."

Calum winced. "He kinda cried. But he didn't say why."

Brix knew, but he kept it to himself, staring some more at the intricate, *soulful* work that belonged on a man like Rubi Matherson.

"How do you know so much about Harvest House?"

Brix blinked, the gnawing sensation returning to his gut as if he hadn't spent all day vanquishing it. "How do you think?"

Calum came back to the table. "You've been there?"

"More than once."

"Why?"

Brix couldn't handle the distress in Calum's eyes. The concern. "Don't look at me like that."

Calum said nothing. Being quiet was his baseline and Brix had learned years ago to let him breathe, but the silence got under his skin, sharpening the words he spoke next.

"Are you going to make me tell you all about it?"

Calum flinched, and it was a stab to Brix's heart.

You're hurting the nicest bloke in the world.

"I—"

Calum cut him off. "You don't have to tell me anything."

"I know." Brix unclenched his fists. "But I think it would be better for both of us if I did."

Calum sat down again, as if he was trying to make himself smaller. "You don't have to tell me any-fucking-thing. I didn't mean to push you there. I'm sorry."

"Fuck, don't do that, Cal. Don't apologise for *my* fuckery. That's not how this goes between you and me. However close we get, you're not my punch bag."

However close we get. What did that even mean? That they weren't close already? That years of dormant friendship and two drunk kisses didn't mean fuck all without *this*?

Christ, Brix didn't even know how Calum felt about *Rob*, and the idea that Calum was still in love with the arsehole who'd driven him all the way to Porth Ewan made him want to puke.

"Hey." Calum reached across the table and rubbed Brix's shoulder. "It's okay."

"You don't know that."

"Then tell me...if you want to. Or don't. I'm not going anywhere."

You don't know that either. But words tumbled out of Brix before the thought solidified. "I got sectioned when I was fourteen. My brother found me in the shed with a noose around my neck."

Horror darkened Calum's features. For the third time in five minutes, he asked Brix, "*Why?*"

Brix drifted, trying to remember. "I heard my dad say he'd shoot a *fag* on sight rather than drink with one. It fucked with my head for a long time, even after Abel found me, until I realised my dad wasn't his words."

Calum's fingers flexed, like he wanted to hold Brix's hand for real. "What do you mean?"

"My dad . . . he's been through a lot himself, you know? He wasn't raised in the world we were. I'm not excusing inbred homophobia, but it nearly killed him when the social worker told him I was scared of him. He came to the ward that night with a bottle of scrumpty-dumpty and told me he'd be proud to share his cider with me, even if I did like it up the arse."

Calum's eyes widened. "He said what?"

Brix laughed, relief flowing out of him, though he'd barely scratched the surface. "Don't be hard on him. It was as much as he could ever give me. My lot ain't never gonna win any diversity contests. They are who they are, and they allow me the same privilege. Can't ask for more."

"I don't know what to say." Bewilderment still creased Calum's face in sharp lines that didn't suit him. "The stuff about your dad makes sense, but I can't believe I never knew that part of your coming-out story. I thought you'd just had a rough few weeks with your brother."

"Nah, Abel was cool. The up the butt thing freaks him out, but find me a straight bloke who doesn't lose his balls at the thought of riding dick."

Calum finally smiled. "There's plenty of gay blokes can't handle it either."

"Not you, though."

"Not me."

Because Calum liked to bottom. Brix remembered that years old conversation. Maybe? Regardless, an image of Calum straddling his waist, strong thighs holding Brix in place, invaded Brix's mind with such fucking force that he had to take a breath. A startled snatch of air that had Calum frowning again.

"What's wrong?"

"What?"

"You've been weird all week."

"Sorry."

"Fuck, don't do that." Calum repeated Brix's earlier words with a soft grin. "I can handle anything as long as you're okay."

"I'm okay," Brix lied. "You want some lunch?"

"Lunch?"

"Yeah." Brix stood, naked Calum fading and the bleach scent of Harvest House returning full force. "I'll be back in a bit."

He fled before Calum could answer and did what all Lusmoores did when the world closed in on him—he ran to the sea. To the cliffs and the caves. And he stayed there until he could breathe again.

CHAPTER
ELEVEN

Calum woke with a jump, heart racing, breath caught in his chest.

He sat up, gaze pinging around the dark room, aware that whatever had startled him was likely a cat, but freaked out all the same. His chaotic life with Rob had left him a light sleeper, attuned to every sound of someone sneaking in or out. Every quiet click and creak of a house that should've been sleeping.

The metallic scrape of Brix's back gate.

Calum frowned and reached for his phone.

3 a.m.

What the fuck?

Against his better judgement—*mind your own business*—he got up and moved to the window. A shadow caught his eye, and the looming outline of pallet crates. Was he dreaming?

Staring at the shadows gave him no answers. Instinct drew him out of his room and on to the landing, but he hesitated at Brix's bedroom door. He'd been unpredictable since the drunken night neither of them ever mentioned—the scrumpy, the *kiss*. Some days he seemed the happiest bloke in the world.

Others, Calum couldn't tell if his ominous words about the past still held true.

You can come up here wanting to jump...

My brother found me in the shed with a noose around my neck.

Calum shivered on the cold landing. Brix had been suicidal at *fourteen*? Jesus. Calum's clusterfuck with Rob felt more pathetic than ever.

Fuck it.

He knocked on Brix's door. There was no reply. He tapped again, louder, but when he heard nothing, grew a pair, and pushed the door open to Brix's empty bed, sheets rumpled and scattered, clothes littering the floor, like he'd got up in a hurry. Only the navy-blue washbag seemed to be in its place, and unease prickled Calum's skin. He left the cluttered scene behind and padded downstairs, half-expecting to find Brix in front of the dying fire, sipping tea and sketching, like he did most evenings.

But the living room was empty too, and the kitchen. Brix was nowhere to be seen, and for the first time in more than a month, Calum felt truly alone. *Don't like it.* He rubbed his chest, worry squeezing his heart. Brix hadn't said he was going out, and at 3 a.m. where the fuck would he even go?

Calum had no idea, and the unease in his bones kept him from shuffling back to bed and minding his own business.

He stoked the fire, remembering what Brix had taught him about stacking the logs for optimum heat. The flames were hypnotic, but the phantom crates in the garden drew him to his feet again.

Outside, he shivered in the bitter wind that blew in from the sea. The crates were real, solid wood—he checked—though they weren't as tall as he'd imagined. And fuck knew what was in them.

"What are you doing out here?"

Calum spun around.

Brix stepped out of the shadows, eyes dark and hooded. "Missing the wind from your warm bed?"

"Missing you." Calum spoke without thinking. "Not from my bed. From yours. You weren't there when something woke me up."

"Fuck's sake." Brix ran a hand through his wild hair.

"Sorry."

"Not you." Brix stepped closer, hooking two fingers under Calum's chin and coaxing his gaze from the ground. "Don't do that."

"Do what?"

"Look down like you're the fucking problem. You surprised me. I don't hate you."

Brix meant well, but the fierceness in his gaze made Calum's heart race. Or maybe it was his proximity. The heat of his fingers. His ocean scent.

Who knew? Not Calum. He didn't know anything except the hard truth that he should've stayed inside. In bed, in the house Brix was charging him fuck all to live in.

The cold wind made itself known.

Brix shivered and reclaimed his hand. "You shouldn't be out here. It's fucking baltic."

"I'm not going to get any colder than you."

Light flickered in Brix's gaze. "I'm already freezing."

"Then come inside."

"Can't."

To ask *why* burned Calum's chest. He turned his attention to the boxes instead. "What's in these?"

"Dunno. Haven't looked."

"Because…"

"They're not mine." Brix sighed and his faint grin disappeared. "My aunt, Peg. She dumped them here cos she's too tight to pay her gang to lug them up the cliffs to the caves. Reckons I'll get pissed off enough to do it for her . . . and she's right."

The cliff-top cave Brix had disappeared into a few weeks ago flashed into Calum's mind. If Brix was talking about the same one, it meant he'd be lugging the stacked crates up the highest cliff in the town...*on his own.*

Calum eyed the crates. "You've already moved some, haven't you?"

"How can you tell?"

"Because you're knackered, and there's less crates than when I first saw them out of the window. You must have been and gone while I was messing with the fire."

Brix nodded slowly. "This isn't me, you know that, don't you? I have no idea what's in them, or where they came from, I just . . . can't have them here. I'm not part of that world."

"I know." Despite what Calum had yet to learn about the Lusmoore clan, he knew there wasn't an ounce of bad in Brix. "Wait here."

He stepped inside, grabbed his coat, and stamped into his shoes. Back *outside*, he thought he might find Brix already gone, but he remained, staring at the crates in the misty moonlight, his expression inscrutable.

Calum approached, his footsteps quiet on the gravel. "How are we doing this? On foot?"

"You don't have to help."

"If you think I could sleep with you out here, you're out of your fucking mind." In the harsh night air, Calum felt more awake than ever, but Brix was exhausted. "Come on, mate. Let's go."

Daylight Brix might've taken more persuading, but late night Brix shrugged and picked up a box, holding it out to Calum.

Calum took it, inclining his head. "Stick another on."

"No."

"Yes."

The stand-off was short. Brix conceded, loading Calum with another box before hoisting the last onto his shoulder. "It's a fair walk. Let me know if you need to stop."

"I won't."

"What? Ever?"

Calum held Brix's gaze under the light of the moon. "For as long as you need me."

It was Brix who stopped first in the end, at the bottom of the cliff path. "It's fucking windy up there, and the path's slippery. Stay tight, okay? Walk where I walk."

Calum nodded and leaned closer to Brix, raising his voice over the crashing waves. "I can take your box too."

Brix rolled his eyes. "I'm fine. Let's go."

And so they went, scaling the steep cliff path with careful steps, slowed down by the weight of their cargo. Their *heavy* cargo, that Brix had already carried up the cliff alone.

Twice. A strong gust of wind blew Calum off course. He stumbled into Brix's back, causing Brix to stoop low to steady them both.

"All right?" Brix shouted over the wind.

Calum nodded, then remembered Brix couldn't see him. "I'm good. Keep moving."

They pressed on, battling the oncoming gale. The cold

seeped into Calum's bones, freezing his joints and numbing his fingers. Twenty feet from the cave, it began to pour a hard, driving rain that soaked his clothes, plastering his jeans to his legs. Wet through, he navigated the final ascent to the cave's entrance, following Brix around the rock and under the ledge, guided by the faint glow of Brix's phone.

Brix dropped his crate on top of the others. Calum followed suit and then took in the murky interior of the cave.

It wasn't what he'd pictured when he'd first seen Brix slip inside all those weeks ago. *Damn.* This wasn't a cave; it was a fucking warehouse. "What is all this?"

Brix covered the new stack of crates with some dusty tarpaulin. "Fuck knows. Most of it comes ashore in the next town over, same as it did back when we were a clan of wreckers."

"Wreckers?"

"Lazy smugglers. Thieves. The Lusmoore gangs lurked on the cliffs in bad weather, and falsely guiding ships into the rocks, wrecking them so they could loot when the storm cleared. Made my ancestors a tidy fortune, until my great-grandad lost it all."

"Wow." Porth Ewan was like nowhere Calum had ever been. "How does that link to now?"

Brix shrugged. "It don't, 'cept my lot are still a bunch of pirates. They just bring the stuff ashore themselves these days. Got contacts in the shipping world, pals in Ireland and France. All in with the biker gangs, before I begged Rubi to cut them off. All sorts end up in my garden before some mug lugs it here, and to the other caves Peg's cousin has a little ways over."

Again with the biker gangs. Calum recalled the sleeping man he'd inked and tried to marry that with the stereotype dancing through his wild imagination, but even though he'd come in with split knuckles and bruises, it was hard to picture Rubi anything but fast asleep on his table. "How often do you have to do this?"

"Once a month, sometimes more, depending on the tides. It's always Peg who drops me in it. Her crew went to shit when her fella got sent down, and she reckons if she dumps loot in my yard, she won't have to get it up here herself. And she's not wrong. I can't have this crap anywhere near me. I've got a business to run, people who depend on me." Brix's expression fractured. "I can't live that life—it would kill me."

Can't lose him.

That thought was louder than any other. In the cramped space, Calum moved closer. "Can't pick your family, eh?"

A shadowy grin warmed Brix's face. "Nope. Thanks for helping me, though. There's no one else I'd trust."

"Nowhere else I'd rather be."

Brix's smile expanded, but a vicious gust of wind broke the moment. "Come on. Let's get home before your city bones freeze to death."

"I'm okay."

"Okay isn't good enough."

Calum didn't know what that meant. He followed Brix out of the cave and down the rocky cliff path. The promise of imminent warmth felt like Christmas come early, but he couldn't deny the magic he'd felt holed up in the cave with Brix, like it was the two of them against the world. Brix had saved him, in more ways than one, and the idea that maybe he'd repaid a tiny fraction of his friendship was too good to leave behind.

Shame the wind and driving rain had other ideas. For most of their descent, it was all Calum could do to keep his head up and follow Brix's sure-footed lead, which left him to the mercy of his mind, replaying the tale Brix had told him in the cave.

He caught up with Brix at the next bend. "Is this what your brother went to prison for? The family business?"

Brix cast an unreadable glance over his shoulder. "No. Abel was even less involved in it than I am. Ironic, eh?"

"There's no irony if you don't have a choice."

"Yeah, well. Abel would've tossed it out on the street, left it for the old bill to find and do whatever they'd do with it. He didn't give a fuck about family loyalty. He had his own life."

Brix turned and kept walking.

Calum followed, warring with indecision. Brix seemed in the mood to talk, but he'd had years to tell him—to tell anyone in London—why his brother was in a Cat-A prison, and he never, ever had.

Leave it alone.

Calum swallowed a thousand questions and pressed on.

Ten minutes later, Brix stopped dead and spun around.

"Abel's nothing like my dad and my uncles, or Peg and me. We didn't even know he had the Lusmoore temper until the coppers came to tell us he'd beat some bloke to death at the side of the M4."

The rumours were true. Calum's breath caught in his throat. "He killed someone? Why?"

Brix shrugged, walking again, Calum beside him now the path had widened. "Road rage? Who the fuck knows? His girl-friend ran off with his best mate the day before, so it could've been that, or any of the Lusmoore shite he'd lived through, but I ain't ever been convinced he meant to kill anyone."

"You don't think he had it in him?"

"More that the evidence pointed to an accident. The bloke hit his head on the road when he went down. But because he was a rich kid driving a fucking Lexus, and Abel was a Lusmoore, none of that mattered. Abel was a champion boxer and they said in court he'd have known how much damage he could do with one punch. Didn't matter that he hadn't been in trouble since he was fifteen. They did him for twelve years."

"Twelve years?" Calum whistled. "And he's got two left?"

"Thereabouts. He could've been out sooner, but he's never applied for early release."

"Why not?"

"Guess he doesn't want to come home. Speaking of, you can see the shop from here, look."

Calum followed Brix's gaze inland to the seafront. Beyond the main promenade, he could just make out the neon lights that lit up Blood Rush when the studio was closed, Brix's house further on.

They kept walking, the silence between them loaded and hot, distracting Calum from the cold until they reached the cottage twenty minutes later.

Brix made straight for the fire.

Calum made tea and took it to him. "Can I ask you something?

Brix glanced up, eyes hooded and weary. "Can't promise an answer if it's pirate related. Don't think there's much left I can tell you without walking the plank."

"It's about what you said about wanting to jump from the cliffs. It made me wonder if what happened when you were a kid had happened again."

"You wanna know if I've tried to top myself since?"

Physical pain twisted Calum's gut. "I guess."

Brix held Calum's gaze for a long moment before he turned back to the fire. "The simple answer is no. I've never done anything like that since that one time, but I'd be lying if I said

I'd never thought about it. It's in me, you know? In my blood. Lusmoores can't deal with life without turning the sea black."

"Depression?"

"No . . . jumping off cliffs. My sister was ten years older than me. She offed herself when I was nine."

Calum blinked. "What?"

"You didn't know that?"

"Only that she died. You never said how." Calum gave up on his crouch and parked his arse on the floor. "Was I that hard to talk to back then? That self-absorbed?"

"Cal, don't torture yourself over my bullshit. It ain't worth it."

"I reckon it is."

"So? I reckon whatever's put yourself-esteem in a skip fire is worth me jumping on a train back to London and kicking the shit out of your dickhead ex, but I've gotta live with that, cos I can't see you letting me do it."

"That's not the same thing."

"Isn't it?"

"Rob never did anything that matters."

Brix's eyes blazed. "He hurt you. Don't think I don't see you flinch every time a door slams at the studio. Or Kim's shouting cos he's lost something."

Calum turned away, gaze fixed on the wall, certainty roiling through him. Brix's sister had *killed herself*. Brix had wanted to die too—more than once. How did anything that had happened in Calum's life compare to that?

Simple. It didn't. "You're wrong," he whispered.

Brix's only answer was to lie down on the floor and sleep, hand over his stomach, face hidden in the crook of his elbow, while Calum stared.

The hand on Brix's abdomen bothered him. He'd seen it all

week, as if Brix's hangover had never quite gone. *There's more.*
To Brix's story. So much more, but Calum wasn't sure how
much he could take before every horrible thing that had
happened to Brix tore his heart in two.

He got up to make breakfast. Feed the chickens and raid
the egg stash, moving slowly to give Brix more time.

Then he got worried that sleeping on the floor would do
more harm than good, and crouched to wake him. "Brix?"

Brix's groan was tortured. "Hmm?"

"Breakfast. You need to eat before work."

"Fucking hell." Brix shifted, opening his eyes. "You're an
actual, real life angel."

"If you like your angels washed up and poor."

"I like *you*."

Calum liked Brix too. More than that. But without the balls
to say so, all he had was two plates of egg-on-toast.

Brix disappeared upstairs.

He came back ten seconds later and necked a mug of cold
tea, when Calum happened to know Brix thought cold tea was
the worst abomination on earth.

"You want a hot one?"

"Nah. Let's eat."

They fell on their breakfast. Calum watching Brix in case he
slid back into sleep where he sat. "I can open the studio for
you. Your bookings don't start till ten."

"How do you know that?"

"My name's below yours on the computer."

"If you ever put your face in that thing and understand it,
you're weeks ahead of me." Brix cleared his plate and pushed
it away. "And thanks for the offer, but I've got one of the bikers
coming through first thing for a touch-up. He's hard to nail
down, so I don't want to put him off."

"He a friend of yours?"

Brix shrugged. "As much as Rubi is. We lead different lives, but we have history. I used to tattoo his dad, and Rubi's. They're both dead now—fuck, have I told you a single anecdote without someone dying?"

Not recently, but Calum kept that to himself and took the plates to the sink. Yawning. Rinsing. Watching the chickens dance in the dirt as lean, tattooed arms slid around him, stilling his busy hands.

Brix.

"Cal," he whispered. "I need you to know that if I was gonna tell anyone my darkest secrets, it would be you."

Calum closed his eyes, absorbing the bone-warming heat of Brix's chest against his back. "There's always more, isn't there?"

"For both of us. What I'm really saying is I wish you trusted me too."

Brix was gone before Calum could answer.

CHAPTER
TWELVE

Chaos surrounded Brix. Mostly his own, but that didn't make it less annoying. "Where's the fucking printer ink?"

Lee ignored him, eyes on her work, following *his* sacred instruction to never let anything distract her when she put a needle to skin.

Kim wasn't tattooing. He was fucking about with driftwood and paint, but he had no sensible answers either. "Ask Lena."

"Your girlfriend isn't here."

"Girlfriend? Who's that?"

Brix growled and stomped to the storeroom, turning it upside down before Lee intervened.

"What are you doing?"

"You know what I'm doing. I'm looking for the printer ink like I have been all fucking day."

"It's up there."

Lee pointed to the only shelf Brix hadn't torn apart. To the box of ink sitting pretty with the rest of the office supplies. "Did something crawl up your arse and die?"

"Go away."

"Are you hangry?"

"Fuck *off.*" Brix pushed her out of the room and shut the door.

Then forgot why he was in the storeroom in the first place. Hmm. Maybe he was hungry, but it wouldn't be because he'd missed breakfast. Despite claiming he couldn't cook for shit, Calum had made him breakfast every morning since their witching hour cave run.

I could get used to that.

Fuck. He already had. Just like everyone else. Lee, Kim, Lena. They all loved Calum. How could they not?

How could anyone hurt him?

Brix's temper burned bright again. He glared at the printer ink, trying to remember what he'd needed it for.

He was still trying when the storeroom door cracked open and Calum peered round it, hair tousled from the wind, a Blood Rush tee clinging to his shoulders enough that Brix forgot just about everything and *stared.*

Calum smiled, shyness creeping into his eyes, a glimmer of sunshine on a cold winter's day, until Brix noticed the bandage on his hand.

"What happened to you?"

Guilt made an unwelcome return to Calum's face. "The gun kinda blew up on me this morning. Took the skin off my fingers. Sorry, mate. I'll replace it."

"As if I give a shit about the gun. Did you let Kim check it out? He's good with blood."

"You're not?" Calum tugged the edge of the bandage.

Brix backed up so fast he hit the shelves behind him, sending paper and ink clattering to the floor.

"Whoa." Calum stepped further into the room, letting the door swing shut behind him. "What's wrong?"

Brix caught his overreaction and reeled it in, but it was too late to escape Calum's concern. "Did you call the bank back?"

"Yeah. Two hundred a month until the end of time. What's *wrong*?"

"Lena took the day off and the world fell apart."

It wasn't that much of a lie. But it wasn't an answer to the question Calum had asked and it showed on his face. "Do you need to eat something?"

Brix's stomach said no.

His head said yes. "Maybe."

"All right then." Calum opened the door. "I'll be back."

He melted away.

Brix wanted to die. Literally. A split second of self-loathing that drove a tortured groan from his chest, and sent his knuckles flying into the wall, grounding himself in the pain.

Except, it didn't ground him. Because nothing changed. Because he *missed* Calum, and waiting for him to come back made staying alive worth it.

"It's not a dhansak from the Akash in Shoreditch, but the one I scoffed on the way back from the shop was fucking amazing."

Brix raised his head from the box of spare machine parts he'd found himself lost in. "Is that a keema pasty from Belly Acre Farm?"

"You can tell that by smell alone?"

"Me and Kim lived on them for a month when they first started selling them at the street market."

Calum grinned and relinquished the paper bag, along with a tiny jar of mango chutney.

Brix dug in. "Wanna bite?"

"Nope. I was lying when I said I ate one on the way home. It was two."

"What else have you been up to today?"

Brix already knew Calum had been working on the skills he'd been trading with Lee. Her watercolour to his dot work, but he wasn't ready for Calum to leave again. Wasn't ready to lose that soft, sweet smile. The self-conscious way he rubbed his jaw as he painstakingly chose his words.

"It's a slow process. I don't have the balls to freehand like she does."

"Not the same as overthinking every dot?"

"I don't do that." Calum's shy smile turned wry. "Okay, maybe I do, and that's why Lee's struggling with my style— cos she doesn't have the patience."

"Funny that." Brix finished his lunch. "It's almost like you funnelled your personalities into your work."

"Oh yeah? What does that make you and Kim?"

"Boring."

"Lies."

"All right. We're boring compared to *you*. Rubi messaged me this morning asking if Kim would mind if he came to you for his chest piece."

Calum cringed. "I can't take work off Kim."

"You're not. He doesn't want to be here full time anymore. Tattooing isn't the thing that gets him out of bed in the morning."

"It's not?" Calum moved closer, and the door shut behind him again.

We're alone. Somehow, that knowledge made Brix breathe easier.

"Kim likes building furniture," he answered Calum's

unspoken question. "He's just never been together enough to make a living out of it."

"Is that changing?"

Brix shrugged. "Isn't everything?"

The door opened before Calum could answer.

Kim, his curious, smirk too knowing for Brix's scratchy heart. "Your pa's here."

"For fuck's sake. What for?"

"Dunno." Kim glanced between Brix and Calum again. "Maybe he's spent all his pension already."

"In the bookies with yours, eh?"

Kim answered in Cornish.

Brix rolled his eyes and stood. "I'm coming."

He followed Kim to the front of the studio, trying not to obsess over where Calum went next. If he stayed in the storeroom, or slipped out the back door like he sometimes did when he'd had enough peopling for one day.

John Lusmoore waited at the front desk, frowning at Corey's abstract flash. "What in God's name is that?"

"Afternoon to you too," Brix retorted. "I've been looking for you all week. Where've you been?"

"What do you care? Can't a man have a life to 'imself anymore?"

"Not if you want paying."

His father's face brightened. "Got some papers for me, 'av ya?"

"Start of the month, ain't it?" Brix ducked behind the front desk and retrieved the envelope he'd stashed in the till. "If you let me put this in the bank, you'd have had it three days ago."

John Lusmoore took the envelope and stuffed it inside his coat. "Go on with yer."

Brix let it go. Some things didn't need fixing. "How are the chooks?"

"Oh yeah, they're fine." John's hawkish expression softened. "I've put 'em on that organic grain from Hunter's and got that heavy straw in for the winter. Can't have my girls getting cold."

"You want some more? Millstream Poultry are kicking out soon."

"How many you getting?"

"Haven't said I'll do it yet."

"Aye-aye, but you will."

Brix grinned. He had little in common with his father, but in this they were the same. John would be by his side at every rescue if he could be trusted not to lamp the farmers. "You're probably right. But what the fuck am I gonna do with them? Got no space left out back."

Especially with Peg's lot dumping shite in my yard. And John's dark glance told Brix he knew all about the crates that had found their way into Brix's back garden. Probably knew their contents too, which was more information than Brix needed or wanted. "What are you doing later? You want a pint?"

John was still scowling at Corey's flash. "Can do, can do. It's blowing a tewedh out there, mind. Third storm this month. Going to be a big one, let me tell you."

"You do tell me. All the time. It's why Abel calls you Uncle Fish, remember?"

"If you say so. What about that fella you got at your place? He brave enough to come out?"

"Um . . ." Brix's tongue let him down for no discernible reason whatsoever. "Do you want him to come?"

"Up to you, lad. He's not going to get all fisticuffs like that one with the orange hair, is he?"

Brix pursed his lips. "No, and Lee wouldn't have done that if you'd thumped Uncle Nige for her."

John muttered under his breath, but Brix let him be. *He brought fresh eggs for Lee every day after her surgery, remember?* Not that Lee would ever know the mysterious baskets on her doorstep had come from John Lusmoore, or that it was the closest thing to an apology he'd ever made to an emmet.

"I'll be off, then," John said. "Find me later."

"Don't forget to eat dinner before you hit the Bell."

"Piss off, boy."

John left. Brix watched him disappear up the road, but the call to drift back to Calum was too strong to ignore.

He found him setting up for a walk-in Brix hadn't noticed arrive.

"You want to go out tonight?"

"Out?" Calum wrapped cling film around the arm of his client's chair. "Thought you were off the juice?"

"Nah, just can't handle the bangers anymore. I'm meeting my dad for a pint at the Sea Bell. Wanna come?"

Calum had his back to him, sketching a few lines on the design the client had brought in. "You want me to meet your dad?"

"Sure, why not? He's an arsehole, but he means well. Trust me, you won't buy a drink all night."

"What was in the envelope you gave him?"

"What?"

"The envelope. Were you paying him off?"

"Well, he don't take cheques."

Silence, then Calum shook himself. "Sorry. Old ghosts, you know?"

"I know my ghosts, mate. Never met yours."

"Right."

Brix raised an eyebrow. "You okay to work with that hand?"

"Yup."

That was it. Calum had nothing else to say and a client waiting in the tiniest shorts Brix had ever seen.

This place, man. "I'll get a screen."

With tiny-shorts bloke shielded from the rest of the studio, Brix left Calum to his work and retreated to the store room again to brood. He hadn't noticed Calum observing his exchange with John, let alone thought that it might trigger him.

What the fuck did that cunt do to him?

Thinking about it wound Brix up all over again, and without Calum to calm him down, he was fuming by the time Kim came back.

"Man, you should see the piece Calum put on that weird bloke. It's fucking sick."

"What was it?"

"Come and *see.*"

Kim bullied Brix out of the store room, probably the only man on earth who could handle Brix without getting decked. He dragged him all the way to Calum's station before he found himself staring at the freakiest *penis* tattoo he'd ever seen.

"Is that a dragon?"

"That's right." The client beamed. "I'm going to get a Prince Albert to give it eyes."

Calum's broad shoulders shook with silent laughter. He turned away, letting Brix deal with the man, and Brix found himself lost for words. The dragon was amazing. Intricate and clever. But seeing it wrapped around a flaccid cock was more disturbing than he cared to admit.

"It's, er, great," he finally said. "Should get it wrapped up, though. Keep it clean."

He fled to the desk.

Calum joined him, adding the job to Lena's system with zero fumbling. Printing out an invoice from the printer Brix had been so sure had run out of ink.

His body heat left Brix dizzy. Left him yearning for something just out of reach.

Give him more. "I was paying my dad an instalment on the money he loaned me to open this place." Brix startled himself as much as Calum. "I paid it off years ago, but he hasn't noticed, so I'll keep topping up his pension until he does—anyway, it's nothing dodgy, I swear."

"I know." Calum focused on stapling penis man's paperwork together. "Don't humour me."

"Why not? It's not your fault someone fucked you up."

Calum's gaze snapped to Brix. "How do you know? Perhaps it was all my fault. Know my own mind, don't I? No one ever *made* me feel that way."

"Says who? Someone treats you like dirt, it conditions you to believe that you don't deserve any better."

They were interrupted again. Calum's client emerged from the back of the studio, dressed, and brandishing a bundle of cash. Brix waited for Calum to take the payment and the client to leave so they could finish a conversation that wasn't about chickens, food, or ink, but it wasn't to be. Dragon Dick left, but as the door swung shut behind him, it opened again, revealing that Kim had returned with Lena in tow.

Super. Brix glared at Kim, who'd always had a way of reading his mind, but Lena spoke before Kim could react.

"Can I borrow you? I need a favour."

"Better be a good one," Brix followed her back into the studio. "Nice hair."

Lena touched hair that was now her natural rich red. "Thanks. Reckon I'm getting a bit old for a technicolour barnet."

"Bet Kim doesn't think so."

"Well . . . that's not going to matter soon."

"Say what?"

Lena shrugged. "I've got itchy feet. Kim wants to stay around here, but there's someone I'm starting to miss."

"Someone else?"

"Yeah, you know how it is."

"Thought you were banging Cam O'Brian?"

"I am—I *was*. Anyway, I'm not talking about him. Or his friend." Lena's gaze morphed from fond to filthy. "I met someone a while back who wants to travel, and I want to go with them."

"What about Kim?"

"What about him? You didn't see the grin on his face when he came back from that gig the other night? The one *I* didn't go to?"

No. Brix had been too wrapped up in his own shit to notice much of anything. "He met someone?"

"Not yet. But he's going to."

"And you're okay with that?"

"Of course. He's my forever love, but we're not forever *lovers*."

Brix absorbed that as Lena kissed his cheek. Then the rest of it set in with a wave of holy panic. Lena ran Blood Rush with an iron fist. How the fuck was he going to manage without her?

"You'll be all right." Lena squeezed his hands. "We'll find someone to replace me, and Kim will still be here."

"Not with the wood shop taking off."

"He'll still need you, Brix. Don't forget that."

As if Brix ever would. Kim's demons were as loud and rowdy as his own. "I don't know what to say."

"Don't say anything, then. Just tell me how to sign my half of the studio back over to you."

"What?"

Lena folded her arms across her chest. "I can't keep it. Not when I owe you everything in the world for giving it to me in the first place."

"I gave it to you because I needed you to stay with me."

"That was years ago. You need to make room in your life for yourself now, and maybe someone else."

"Yeah?"

"*Yes.*" Lena hugged him again and whispered in his ear. "Someone like Calum, cos I reckon there's room in his universe for you too."

Hearing her say it got under Brix's skin—in a good way, the best—but Brix was too used to the best things in life passing him on by.

The air shifted.

A ripple.

He drew back from Lena, feeling that *pull* again, but when he got back to the front desk, Kim was alone.

"Where's Calum?"

Kim glanced up from carving patterns into the legs of Lena's desk chair. "Dunno. Some dude rang for him, and he shot out of here like his arse was on fire."

"Some dude? Rang where? The studio? Who was it?"

Kim blinked. "Studio phone. Some posh cunt looking for Calum. I passed him the phone and then he was gone."

"Gone where?"

"I don't know."

"You didn't follow him?"

"Why would I do that?"

Brix cursed and ran for the door and outside, dashing to the end of the narrow street. But he found nothing but tourists and seagulls.

Kim was right: Calum had gone.

CHAPTER
THIRTEEN

Brix left the studio behind and ran home, hoping he'd find Calum camped out on the living room floor, staring into a newly built fire. But the cottage was dark and empty, the only sound Zelda's disgruntled yowl as she sashayed around his ankles demanding dinner.

Dennis was nowhere to be seen. Was he upstairs with Calum?

Brix dashed up to check, but the bedroom was empty too, and Dennis was sleeping next to a prized dead mouse in the bathtub.

Fuck.

Head-spinning, Brix disposed of the mouse and washed his hands, scalding his skin under the hot tap as every second he'd spent with Calum in the last month replayed on a loop.

His shy mellow voice and shy smile.

The long-healed bruise on his face and the profound distress in his dark gaze every time his weapons-grade *twat* of an ex came up in conversation

Brix's skin crawled, rage and worry fighting for dominance. Worry won, and unease prickled his skin.

Rob.

He'd hurt Calum, the scars he'd left behind far deeper than Brix could ever see, but he knew that pain. What it did to a man. And where had it taken Brix, each and every time?

Fuck. *Fuck.*

He shut off the tap and ran for the stairs, charging out of the cottage, the door banging shut behind him.

Boots pounding the earth, he made for the cliff path, praying he'd make it to the caves before the storm clouds over the sea came ashore. That he was wrong and Calum had more sense than to climb the cliffs in the rain. But as hard as Brix tried, he couldn't remember if he'd ever given Calum that warning. If it had ever occurred to him that Calum would ascend the path alone, and he fucking *hated* himself. How many lives had these cliffs claimed since Brix had been born? How many in the years and years before?

Calm your tits. He's probably in the pub.

Probably. But Brix's brain loved the dark more than his soul claimed the light, and the terror squeezing his heart choked him.

Literally.

He stopped, doubling over, hands on his thighs, coughing up fear, lungs burning like he'd smoked a thousand cigarettes before tackling a marathon. Like his body couldn't handle a good old panic attack anymore.

Get your shit together.

Find Calum.

Fuck.

Fuck.

Brix took off running again, the seafront a blur as he reached the path, spray from the crashing waves soaking his face.

Ahead, the clouds darkened as the cliffs loomed, daylight all but gone. But the gloom couldn't hide the set of broad shoulders Brix had searched for in every crowd his entire adult life. *Slumped* shoulders, as a lone figure brooded on the bench at the foot of the hidden path.

Relief gifted Brix a surge of fresh energy. He closed the distance between him and Calum in a snatched breath and skidded to a stop at his feet.

Calum raised his gaze from the ground as driving rain began to fall.

His eyes were hollow and the ache in Brix's chest amped up a gear. "All right?"

"Fucking blinding, Brix. Why do you ask?"

"Don't be a dick."

Calum's belligerence held. Then it faltered and self-doubt shattered his features. "Sorry."

"Don't." Brix crouched at his feet. "Just talk to me. Please. Don't go up that path."

"What path?"

Brix jerked his head, unable to voice any of the colloquial nicknames for the uphill track. "It's not safe up there in the dark."

Calum glanced beyond him. "I wasn't going to go up there."

You were. You just didn't know it yet. "You're not sitting on this bench for nothing."

"Aren't I?"

"Fuck no. Not even hard-core Porth Ewan folk do that."

Calum didn't reply, and his gaze returned to the tempestuous sea.

Brix took a chance and reached out, stilling his twisting fingers. "How's your hand?"

"It's fine."

"What did Rob want?"

"What?"

"Kim told me Rob called the studio. I didn't know you were still in contact with him."

"I'm not. He must've seen some of my work on the Blood Rush socials and recognised the style. Fucking ironic, really, cos he never took much notice of it when it was keeping him in wanky hipster suits."

"He tracked you down? What does he want?"

"Dunno. Didn't ask."

"No?" Brix tried to ignore a selfish wave of relief. "You didn't speak to him?"

Calum shook his head. "Nope. Hung up like a pussy and ran away. Fancied a stroll up the cliffs, until I remembered you *already* told me not to go there in the dark without you."

Thank fuck for past me. "You're not a pussy." Brix squeezed Calum's hands, then reluctantly let them go. "There's plenty of people I don't want to talk to."

"Like Jordan?"

Sharper discord stabbed Brix's heart, but he suppressed the instinct to shut it down. How could he expect Calum to confront this bitter shit if he couldn't do the same?

Besides, this was Calum. Quiet. Perceptive. *Observant.* There was no way he hadn't registered Brix's flinch every time Jordan came up. "I can't talk to him . . . Don't think I ever will again, and he knows better than to call me. But if he did, I reckon I'd be up here just like you said. Sometimes only the sea can hear you scream."

"I'm not screaming." Calum shoved his hands in his pockets. "I wish I could, but it won't come out. Shit. That sounds so fucking stupid."

"Not to me."

"Liar."

"Bollocks." Brix dug his fingers into Calum's unyielding thighs, coaxing him to break his stare with the sea. "There's a lot of things in my life I can't tell anyone, even you, but I'm not a liar, Cal. Told you already, ain't got the heart for it."

Calum's gaze hollowed out again. *I've lost him.* But it was a blip. A temporary absence. A sigh rattled past Calum's lips, then he slowly placed his hands over Brix's, twining their fingers together. "I'm sorry."

"Don't—"

"Stop. Let me have that one, okay? I called you a liar and I was wrong. I just…"

"What?"

"It's been a long time since anyone tried to understand me —since *I* last understood me. I've got no idea who I am, but I feel like you already know."

A biting gust of wind punctuated Calum's words, but Brix barely felt it, hypnotised by the sight of Calum's hand on his. By the feel of him—his skin, his pulse thudding through his palm.

Hearts don't beat through your hands. Fact. But Brix didn't need science to know that touching Calum was a biological reaction he couldn't walk away from.

At least, not anytime soon. "You know your own mind, mate. Just gotta let go of whatever—or whoever—has convinced you that you don't."

"Whoever." Calum let the word hang. "If you'd said that a year ago, I'd have laughed in your face, or punched you. I've never let anyone talk shit about him."

"Nothing wrong with that when you're with someone. You

have their back, even if they're a complete knob. That's the point."

"He'd never hit me before—not really, anyway, if that's what you're getting so angry about."

Not really. "I'm not angry."

"Right."

Calum looked away. Brix caught Calum's face and forced him to meet his eye again. "I'm not playing games with you. No lies, remember? I want to understand the hold this bloke has over you. You don't have to hit someone to fuck them up."

"I used to wish he would."

"Why?"

"I'd have known for sure then that he was wrong."

Brix swallowed. Now they were getting somewhere. "Anything he did to hurt you was wrong. Did he control you?"

"Only because I let him."

"Or because he manipulated you. That's not the same thing."

Calum's shrug was unconvinced, but the driving rain and increasing wind blew Brix's response off course.

He squeezed Calum's hands tighter. "Come home with me?"

Calum slow-blinked at the rain. Then at Brix. "Thought you were meeting your dad?"

"He'll be in the boozer all night. Let's get dry first, okay?"

Brix rose, taking Calum with him.

It made sense to let go.

It made sense to hold on, and they walked home side by side, hand in hand, silence cocooning them. But it wasn't weighted. Calum was always quiet and Brix was deep in thought. He hadn't lied to Calum. In the moment Calum had asked, he hadn't been angry. Just worried. Concerned.

Drowning in his growing feelings for a man he'd spent years believing he'd never seen again. But he was angry now. Raging, if he let the devil in him run loose. And how was that fucking fair? Calum needed a friend right *here*. Not a hot-head to jump on the next train to London and kick the shit out of the arsehole who'd done him so wrong.

They reached the cottage.

Calum let them in, holding the door for Brix to pass. "Jesus. You're shaking."

Brix shrugged out of his leather jacket. "This ain't the coat for hiking in the rain. Have we got wood in?"

"I'll get some."

"Your hand—"

"Brix. Sit down."

Brix shivered for a different reason. He kicked his boots off and went to the fireplace. He hadn't got round to sweeping it out, but Calum had, and Brix didn't need tangible flames to feel the warmth of that.

The comfort.

Calum came back and crouched beside him, setting the fire. Lighting it.

The flames flickered and grew, the heat seeping into Brix's cold bones. He groaned, dropping his head, tiredness sweeping over him, recalling the dark days when huddled in front of the fireplace had been the only place he could sleep. How he'd resented the spring. How the long summer months had felt like a curse.

"Come on, mate." Calum helped him up. "Couch."

"Hmm?"

Calum frowned, the lines in his face wearing the lingering bewilderment of years of silence.

Brix yearned to wipe them away. But he couldn't. He'd

speak a thousand Lusmoore secrets before he shared the darkest of his own.

He let Calum steer him to the sofa. Tea appeared. Cake. "The bakery girls still bringing you their leftovers?"

Calum chewed his lip, concealing that shy smile. "That's what Lena keeps telling me. Not sure I believe her. Reckon she's baking them herself just to rib me."

"Doubt she's got the time." Brix swiped a chunk of railway sponge. "I keep her pretty busy, and she's got a lot on her mind right now."

"Kim said she's leaving."

"He told you that?" Kim didn't share with outsiders, but perhaps he saw what Brix saw, maybe they all did. "I don't want her to go. She's practically my mother. I can't handle that computer system on my own."

"You don't want to handle it. There's a difference."

Brix snorted. "Maybe *you* should handle it for me then."

Calum's smile flared again, but it died as the reason they were huddled on the couch in wet clothes swamped them again. He'd never admitted that he'd stayed in Porth Ewan to hide from Rob, but Brix knew it was true, and now Rob had found him . . .

He'll leave.

The cake in Brix's belly turned to dust. Panic gripping him again. *Guilt.* Wanting Calum to stay for his own benefit made him no better than Rob.

"I'll miss her too," Calum said. "But Kim said it would be good for them. That he needs stability more than her, and she needs to run free without worrying about him all the time."

"Sounds like Kim told you more than he's told me in the past year."

Calum shrugged. "He seemed like he wanted to talk, so I listened."

"You're good like that."

"Am I?"

"You're the best."

"Not bad yourself, Lusmoore."

Calum leaned back on the couch, his damp clothes moulding to his body.

Brix craved to peel them off.

But more than that, he had to *know*. "Tell me about Rob?"

Eyes half closed, Calum sighed. "It's hard to articulate without feeling like a pathetic loser."

Brix growled. Wolfish. *Territorial.*

Calum's brows jumped. "All right there?"

"Yeah. Just hate you talking down to yourself."

"Technically, I'm talking to you."

"Calum."

"Brix." Calum bit his lip again. Let it go. "Look, you can tell me it's not my fault as much as you like, but it has to be to some degree. He didn't force me into being a fucking doormat."

"Was it your idea to put the shop in his name?"

"No."

"Or your phone? And what about your flat? Whose name was that in?"

"Mine. He didn't live there, but the rent came from the business account, and he raided it every month, so sometimes it didn't get paid."

"Harsh."

Calum cringed. "That's not the worst of it. I took out a massive loan a month after we met, gave it to him to set up his accountancy business, but he never made the payments. Black

Star paid some of it off when I didn't take a wage, but I'm way behind."

"How big was the loan?"

"Thirty grand."

"What? How the fuck did you secure it?"

"On a bedsit in Hampstead I bought not long after you left."

Brix braced. "What happened to it?"

"I sold it at a loss. Rob didn't like me having something that was just mine."

"Rob's a cunt."

Calum snorted. "I know that now. At the time, I thought he wanted to buy a flat *together*, close to the shop, and maybe buy that premises too. We had plans and it took me a long time to realise he'd made them all up, and by then . . . by then I was in so fucking deep I couldn't see how badly I needed to get out."

"What enlightened you?"

"I caught him getting slammed in my bed."

Brix reared back. "Bastard."

"Nah, still my fault, according to him. Didn't fuck him well enough. Stifled him too."

More curses bubbled up Brix's throat, but Calum had more to say, and Brix let him speak.

"He liked to keep me dangling. In my place. His favourite trick was to promise me a quiet night in, then piss off into town with his mates without telling me. Then he knew I'd be at home waiting on him while he did whatever the fuck he wanted. Win-win for him."

"Why not go out with you?"

Calum drummed his fingers in his knee. "He latched onto me because of the ink, but I'm not as cool as he thought I'd be, so after a while, he quit wanting me around his friends. And I stopped letting it hurt me. Next to everything else, it didn't mean anything."

"Everything means something if it hurts, Cal. It has to, or we ain't fucking human."

"I didn't feel too human when you found me on that bench. Rob had me tied in knots. I wasn't eating, sleeping, or even thinking straight. It's mad that I was still putting ink on people. It scares me now—I see how unhealthy it was, but back then, I thought I loved him."

Calum choked on the word.

Brix got up and moved to the window. "What about now? You still love him?"

Calum made a low sound. "Not even close. Being with you again has shown me that."

Being with you again has shown me that. Brix's heart thudded, want and need swirling in his chest before he could lock it down. But there was disbelief too. How had Brix shown him anything when all he'd done since Calum had come to Porth Ewan was get drunk, moody, and jam his foot in his mouth?

"I feel like it was never real," Calum whispered.

Brix spun around.

"With Rob," Calum clarified.

"It was real. And it meant something, even if it was nothing more than a hard fucking lesson."

"Is that how you feel about Jordan?"

"I don't feel shit about Jordan." Brix's voice lowered to a gravelled snap. *Fuck.* He returned to the couch and tried again. "I *try* not to feel anything for him, but it's hard when the damage someone leaves behind makes you who you are."

Calum rubbed his hands on his damp jeans. "You're a bigger man than me."

"Not likely, I've just been around enough hate and anger to know it doesn't heal us."

"Your family?"

"We're an angry bunch."

"*You're* not." Calum shifted on the couch. His leg brushed Brix's knee and sent shockwaves through Brix's already tingling nerves. "You were always the one who could make me smile. I missed that when you left."

"What about now? Do I still make you smile?"

Dryness laced Brix's tone, but Calum's answering grin was dazzling. "I reckon so. Rob's mates used to say I had a face like a constipated undertaker. See what happens when you're not around?"

"Telling me shit like that isn't a good way of proving I'm not a rage demon." Brix forced a smile, so Calum wouldn't think he was angry with *him*. So he wouldn't know what he would give to load a van with Abel and Kim and—

No.

That would make him no better than Rob, but the fantasy was more soothing than Brix wanted to admit to Calum's sweet face.

"What are you thinking?"

"Hmm?" Brix blinked to find Calum had shifted closer to study Brix's face.

Brix shoved all thuggish thoughts aside and forced his smile wider. "I'm thinking that I don't want you to go back to London."

"London?" Calum tilted his head to one side. "I haven't thought about going back. But I haven't thought about where I'd go instead."

"You don't need to *go* anywhere. I've been counting on you singing to Bongo my whole fucking life."

Calum pursed his lips. "I don't sing to Bongo. I talk to her, and you know she answers me."

Brix laughed. "She's a keeper, I'll give you that. Best layer of all the new girls. The others are too busy trying to escape."

Calum smiled, for real this time. It warmed every inch of his beautiful face and Brix couldn't look away, basking in the lighter air between them. He still raged at the shame lingering in Calum's dark gaze, but his heart felt Calum's quiet presence like a second skin, and the urge to beg Calum to stay tied him in knots.

Like he'd read Brix's mind, Calum leaned forward and touched Brix's arm, sliding his warm hand over Brix's skin. "Brix?"

"Hmm?"

"I don't want to go back to London."

"Then don't. Stay here."

"Here?"

Brix covered Calum's hand with his own and turned to face him. "*Yes*. Stay here with me. There's a job for you at the studio as long as you want it, and . . ."

"And what?"

"I *want* you to stay, in case I wasn't clear before."

"Why?"

To anyone else, the answer to Calum's question would've been obvious, but Brix had learned that Calum needed to hear these things explicitly to believe them.

I don't want to be without you.

The words were on the tip of his tongue, but as he took a breath, Calum moved again, his face suddenly inches from Brix's, his eyes so dark, his mouth so close. "I—"

Their lips met in a gentle kiss, so soft and light it stole Brix's breath. Head spinning, he opened his mouth to the tender, mind-blowing sweep of Calum's tongue, and his fingers, unbidden, found their way to Calum's velvet beard.

He dragged his nails through it. Calum groaned, deepening the kiss. He wove a hand into Brix's hair and tangled it in the damp mess of windswept waves, twisting and tugging, the sensation a lightning bolt to Brix's dick.

Brix hardened. Heat pooled in his groin. He sucked in a harsh breath, but as the scrape of air filled his lungs, reality crashed into him. What the fuck was he doing? He and Calum had kissed before—more than once—but each time it had been over before it had truly begun, leaving it all too easy to pretend it had never happened, and that the prospect of it going further was nothing but a long-dead dream.

This is different.

Brix reared back as a thud at the door startled Calum too. For a moment, they stared at each other. Calum's intense gaze was tough to read, and Brix couldn't tell if he'd sensed the shift in the air before the pounding had interrupted the inevitable slide into a clusterfuck he had no desire to ever explain.

Then the knocking came again, loud, insistent, and impossible to ignore, breaking the moment.

Brix started to get up.

Calum stilled him. "I'll get it."

He got up and went to the door, as chill as Brix had ever seen him, as if pure *mayhem* wasn't erupting in Brix's soul. He stopped before opening it, though, and looked back, shooting Brix a quizzical frown as thunder clapped outside.

It took Brix far too long to realise he was asking if it was okay to answer the door. He swallowed his frustration and nodded, willing his wayward dick to retreat to its cave before his brain exploded. "You live here too."

"I guess I do." Calum opened the door. The sight of whoever greeted him made him smile, but the light in his face was brief as he stepped back and waved Kim inside.

Brix stood, the party in his jeans and the wake in his heart forgotten as he met the troubled gaze of one of his oldest friends. "What is it?"

"The lifeboat's going out to a stricken tanker."

"What?"

"They're launching now."

Ten years ago, under the cloud of a storm as fierce as the one blowing outside, Kim's words would've filled Brix with horror, because a decade ago the youngest man in Porth Ewan's lifeboat crew had been Abel Lusmoore. But Abel had been gone a long time, and there'd been no Lusmoore in the boat since. "Shit. Did your old man go out?"

Kim shook his head. "No, he's down in Porth Luck at my nan's. That's what I came to tell you. They were a man short, so your dad took his place."

CHAPTER
FOURTEEN

Calum stood by the door in the lifeboat station, shoulder to shoulder with throngs of Porth Ewan folk he'd never seen before. Men, women, children. Old and young. Where the fuck had they all come from?

Then he remembered he spent most of his time in the studio, or at home with Brix and his menagerie. He hadn't mixed much with the locals. *I haven't even met his dad.* And given the haunted faces around him, there was a real possibility he wouldn't get the chance.

Calum glanced at Brix by the control centre with Kim, listening intently to an RNLI officer, like he had been since they'd shouldered their way into the crammed station. Face drawn, eyes tight with worry. Calum wanted more than anything to stand with him, but Kim was there instead, his hand on Brix's shoulder, nodding to things Calum didn't understand as Brix brought both hands to his head, looking for all the world like the worst had already happened.

Something inside Calum snapped.

Fuck this emmet shite.

He pushed off the wall he'd been leaning against and

strode across the crowded room. Kim saw him coming, squeezed Brix's arm, then stepped aside, like he'd been expecting Calum to take his place all along.

Calum dropped into the seat next to Brix and leaned in close. "What's going on?"

Brix met Calum's gaze with a tense frown. "The boat's still out."

Calum had figured that much, but gestured for Brix to elaborate. "Why? What's happened?"

"Explosion on a tanker a few miles out. They're taking on water. The mayday came through an hour ago."

"Why did your dad go? I didn't know he was part of the crew."

"He's a reserve," Brix said hoarsely. "S'posed to be retired, but Kim's old man wasn't there, and the only other able seaman was Sol Bosanko, and no one was going to let him get on that boat with his dad already skippering."

"Why not?"

"Look around you," Brix said. "Look at their faces. Can you imagine waiting here knowing there were two generations of your family at sea on a night like this? It wouldn't be right. Dad and Abel never went out together in a storm."

Calum swallowed. He hadn't taken much notice of the lifeboat station, or the RNLI stickers in every shop window. It had all seemed like part of the furniture. He'd never stopped to wonder why they were there, or what it meant to the local folk. "What happens now?"

"We wait," Kim said when Brix failed to answer. "It's gonna be a long night even if they make the rescue. The boat's only got room for six survivors, and there's twenty-two crew on board the tanker."

"Are there no more boats?"

Kim's gaze darkened. "Porth Luck used to have a bigger vessel, but it got wrecked four months ago. Lost two men. They ain't raised the funds to replace it yet."

Who the fuck paid for lifeboats? Calum had no idea. "Is there nothing else that can help?"

"The Sea King is up in the sky," Kim said. "But they can't winch anyone up in this wind. That boat is the only chance that tanker crew has got. If the *Bonnie Sue* can't get to them, they'll go down with the ship."

"What's the tanker called?"

"*Black Star.*"

Calum's heart stilled. "What?"

But Kim's attention had been diverted by activity on the control screen. He leaned forward. Calum expected Brix to do the same, so Brix's cool hand in his startled him.

"I could sit here all night and not have a fucking clue what they're talking about."

"Yeah?" Calum glanced at the convoluted dash of flashing lights and coordinates. "Not much of a sailor?"

"Hell no. Even a dinghy makes me hurl."

Brix looked pretty close to puking on dry land. Calum squeezed his hand. "Can I get you anything? Call anyone for you?"

If the word on the street was anything to go by, the Lusmoore clan was huge. Surely they'd want to know one of their own was out at sea?

But Brix shook his head. "Anyone who wants to know will by now. They'll come in their own time, or not—I don't give a shit, to be honest. I could do with some air, though. Come with me?"

"Of course."

Hands still clasped, they made their way out of the station

and onto the sheltered rocky outpoint. Calum shivered. They were safe from the rain, but the wind was still vicious, biting and cruel, reminding them, as if they could forget, that the men on the boats were facing far worse.

Brix shuddered too. Calum pulled him close and absently kissed his hair. Brix froze, but it was brief enough for Calum to wonder if he'd imagined it, before Brix gave in and rested his head on Calum's chest with a heavy sigh.

"I don't even like my dad most days. I love him, because he's my dad, and I respect him as much as he deserves, but I don't like him. If he wasn't my father, I'd think he was a cunt."

"Why?"

"'Cos he's the same backward, racist, sexist arsehole he's always been." Brix sighed again. "And he liked Abel better. Still does. Reckon he's counting the days till he gets out and he's not stuck in the pub with me anymore."

"Thought he told you he was proud to have a pint with you?"

"He did. He *is*. Don't mean we've got jack-shit in common. We only ever talk about chickens."

A flashing light in the distance caught Calum's attention. "Is that them?"

Brix peered in that direction. "Nah. That's a ferry."

How he could tell, Calum had no idea, and his chance to ask was interrupted by Kim.

"Just got word they've got the first lot of crew off. Taking them into Porth Luck before they go out again. It's gonna be a long night, Brix. Go home. Sleep. I'll check in every half hour, I swear."

Calum half-expected Brix to refuse, but he didn't. He nodded slowly, then detached himself from Calum to embrace Kim. "You'll call me?"

"Every half hour. Before, if anything changes."

Calum didn't miss the fact that Kim offered no reassurance that everything would be okay. He wondered if the Porth Ewan boat had lost men before, or if the crew who'd perished in the next town along had been friends. Everyone seemed to know everyone in Porth Ewan. Who knew how far that stretched?

Calum nodded farewell to Kim and followed Brix to the footpath that led back to the main town. The cottage was a ten-minute walk away, but it seemed to pass in a flash, and he barely noticed that they were both soaked to the skin . . . again.

Inside, they peeled off damp outer layers and hung them by the fire. Brix poked at the embers, his gaze distant. Calum moved to the kitchen. He was far from hungry, but if Kim's prophecy proved true, Brix needed to eat.

He found pasties and a jar of Branston, and took them to the living room.

Brix looked up and managed a thin smile. "You made dinner?"

"Nah, someone else did. Probably just as well, eh?"

"You can cook. Just don't know it yet."

"Righto. Want tea?"

"I'd rather have a whiskey."

"I can fix that."

Brix shook his head as Calum set the plates on the coffee table. "Don't reckon I'd stop at one. Sit down, mate. I'll make the tea in a bit."

They ate in silence. The pasties were good, but they were lost on Calum as he forced them down, and he imagined it was ten times worse for Brix. Unable to watch him struggle, and despite Brix's spiritless glare, Calum got up and made the tea anyway.

"Thanks." Brix accepted his mug and pushed his plate away. "I don't know what I'd do without you these days."

"Whatever you did before. It's me that needs my arse wiped."

Brix snorted, but his humour faded, and for the dozenth time since Kim had thumped seven bells out of the front door, Calum saw how tired he was.

"Kim told you to get some sleep."

"Who died and put him in charge—" Brix shuddered. "Don't answer that."

He got up and stomped to the foot of the stairs, peeling off his T-shirt as he went and tossing it in the vague direction of the kitchen.

Calum prepared himself to let him go, his gaze lost in the web of intricate ink on Brix's back, then Brix turned, his hand on the bannister, and fixed Calum with a stare that set his every nerve on fire. "You coming, or what?"

Or what never crossed Calum's mind. He hung his own damp T-shirt over the bannister and followed Brix upstairs. On the landing, he hovered at Brix's open door, but Brix's heavy sigh pulled him forward.

"You look like you're being lured into the lion's den." Brix flopped down on his neat bed. "It ain't scary in here, I promise."

"I'm not in here much, eh?"

That wasn't it, but Calum let it go. "You want more tea?"

"Nah, but Cal?"

"Yeah?"

"Sit down. You're making me nervous."

Biting his lip, Calum sat on the edge of the bed.

Brix sat up and mirrored his pose, their shoulders touching. "I know it don't make no sense to you, but this room is my perspective. What I need to wake up to. Tidy space, tidy mind? It's the only way I can cope sometimes."

The theory made sense. Back in London, how many nights had found Calum counting stock that didn't need to be counted? Organising shelves that no one gave a shit about?

Too many, but Black Star Ink had been like that, a world away from the nuclear family of Blood Rush. A world away from *Brix*.

Black Star. Calum's stomach turned over. He reached for Brix, but Brix was already halfway into his arms. "I wish I could tell you it's going to be okay."

"It's all right that you can't." Brix rubbed Calum's jaw with his own. "I don't need you to fix things. It's enough that you're here."

"Why?"

A whisper.

In answer, Brix grasped Calum's face and kissed him deeper than they'd ever kissed before. Hotter. Harder. And with more purpose than Calum could stand if one of them pulled away.

He closed his hands around Brix's, like he could hold Brix to him and never let go. He leaned closer, knocking Brix off-balance so they tumbled to the mattress, and Brix pushed him onto his back, his strong and slender legs pinning Calum in place.

Brix kissed Calum again. And *again*, ploughing his tongue into Calum's mouth until Calum fought his dominance and flipped them over, covering Brix with his heavier weight.

Calum broke the kiss, breathing hard, and dropped his forehead to Brix's, pressing them together like he could force his way into Brix's mind. "What do you want? What do you need?"

"I need to touch you."

"Do it, then."

"I don't want to do it for me. I need you to *want* me. Even if it's just for now. If it's just—"

Calum placed his hand over Brix's mouth and unbuckled

his own belt, rising up on his knees to shove his jeans and boxers down his hips. To let his cock spring free, inches from Brix's face. "I want you. I've *always* wanted you. How can you not know that?"

"You never told me."

"You never asked."

"Because I wanted you too . . . " Brix mauled his bottom lip. "So badly I was afraid of it."

Calum didn't believe that. Then the thought imploded. Brix was the toughest bloke he'd ever met, but in the past month, he'd learned that he was as fragile as anyone. Perhaps *more*. "Don't be afraid. Just touch me, Brix. It'll be okay, I promise."

The uncertainty in Brix's gaze hurt Calum's heart. He grasped Brix's hand and placed it on his dick, holding it there, so Brix could absorb how badly Calum wanted him. It had been so long since anyone had touched him this way, and as Brix's fingers traced a shaky path along his shaft, he wondered how long it had been for Brix. The Brix of old had jumped from bed to bed around Camden, with and without his some-time-lover, Jordan, but he was a different man now, and Calum couldn't believe the tremor in his hands was all about him.

As if.

But Calum gritted his teeth and silenced the devil on his shoulder. Brix's tentative touch was enthralling, consuming, and as it grew in confidence, Calum couldn't look away.

Brix closed his fist around Calum's cock, gentle at first, but then squeezing tighter, and twisting, and *fuck*, grazing his balls with the other hand.

Calum dropped his chin to his chest with a low groan. Long minutes passed in a haze of laboured breaths. Of hypnotic sensation. Orgasm rushed up on him, and he couldn't find the willpower to fight it, or care enough to try as

Brix gripped him harder, abandoning Calum's balls to dig his nails into Calum's hip.

"You're so fucking hot."

You should see yourself. But Calum didn't have the coherency to voice it. Release smashed into him, and he came on Brix's chest with a guttural cry.

"*Fuck.*" Calum fell forward into Brix's waiting arms. "Fuckfuck*fuck.*"

"They'd better be good fucks." Brix wrapped his arms around Calum, smearing the sticky mess between them.

"They're good fucks," Calum croaked. "Lemme touch you too."

He reached for Brix's *rigid* dick, but Brix dodged his hands. "Don't worry about me."

Lethargy washed over Calum like a bellyful of Valium. He grumbled. Maybe? He couldn't be sure. He rolled off Brix and pressed into his side, hooking a leg over his abdomen. "I'm supposed to be looking after you," he murmured as Brix's rough fingertips brushed back his sweat-dampened hair.

"You are," Brix whispered. "More than you know."

It was still dark when Calum woke sometime later. He opened his eyes, and the unfamiliar mattress beneath him felt like his old bed back in London.

Running off like a jilted fucking bride? Don't bother telling stories about me. No one will believe you.

Calum bolted upright, colliding with a bony mass. "*Shit.*"

"Easy." Brix steadied him with one hand, tossing the washbag that lived on his bedside table with the other. In the dim lamp light, his gaze seemed empty and the events that had led to them being holed up in Brix's bed together hit Calum like a train.

He found his equilibrium and grasped Brix's forearm, wrapping his fingers around the slender bones to claim his place in the world. "Did Kim call?"

"A few times. They haven't capsized yet."

"That's good, right?"

Brix swallowed and rubbed his jaw, like he had something stuck in his throat. "They're still pulling crew from the tanker, and it's *still* storming like Mother Nature's bitchy aunt, so you tell me."

Calum regarded Brix; he seemed more irritated that distressed. "You okay?"

"Can't sleep."

"Wanna try?" Calum opened his arms. "I can listen for the phone."

"That ain't how I dreamed of falling asleep on you."

Calum put his hands on Brix's shoulders and tugged him close, then lowered them both to the mattress, his arms closing around Brix, like he could cage him, shelter him, heal him. *I wish.* "We can dream tomorrow when everyone's safe. Just rest for now, even if you can't sleep."

Brix closed his eyes.

Then his heavy sigh broke the storm-punctuated silence, and he sat up, glaring at something unseen beyond the window. "I can't fuck you."

"What?"

Brix tore his gaze from the beating rain and stared at Calum in the darkness. "I meant it when I said I'd wanted you for years—still want you, so fucking much—but I can't have sex with you."

"I—uh. Why not?" It wasn't what Calum meant to say, but

as he uttered the words and Brix's features hardened, the answer felt like a slow death. "Brix?"

"Don't."

"Hey—"

"I *can't*, okay? I just fucking can't. Not with you, not with anyone."

"But—"

"Calum." Brix whispered his name, but the terror lacing every syllable was deafening, and Calum's heart skipped a beat, absorbing the fear and defeat that screamed from every facet of Brix—his slumped shoulders and hung head, his clenched fists and screwed-up eyes.

"Brix, please. Talk to me."

A lifetime passed before Brix opened his eyes, but anything he might've said was cut off by the *Pugwash* theme tune blaring out of his phone. He dove across Calum to snatch it from the pillow beside them. "Dad? Where are you?"

Relief surged through Calum. Unless Brix's father was calling to say goodbye from the upturned hull of a sinking lifeboat, they were about to get some good news.

He slid from the bed, searching out his clothes that were scattered around the room as he listened in on Brix's end of the conversation. Not much made sense from Brix's limited contribution, but the tension easing from Brix's taut muscles spoke a thousand words. Whatever else was going on behind the storm in Brix's eyes, the men at sea were safe.

Brix hung up. "The boat is in. Took the last crew from the tanker into Porth Luck and landed there."

"Where's your old man?"

"In the pub they opened up as a reception centre, drinking the pumps dry like nothing's happened."

Maybe to Brix's father it hadn't. He hadn't seen the torment marring Brix's beautiful face, the pain still dancing around the wall that had sprung up between him and Calum.

"Maybe you'd better go find him, then." Calum spoke around the lump in his throat. "Bring him home."

Brix nodded slowly, like he had so much more to say, but he said nothing, and silence reigned as Calum retrieved his clothes from the floor and pulled them on.

As he left Brix alone and retreated to the bathroom.

He was in the shower when the front door slammed and the van rumbled to life. Both sounds seemed so final that Calum's blood ran cold, despite the steaming spray battering him, washing all traces of Brix from his skin. He laid his head on the tiles, searching for some perspective in the chaos of the last twenty-four hours, but none was forthcoming. Rob's phone call had driven him to the foot of Brix's cliff, but that moment seemed so far away now. As if Calum had become someone else since then.

Someone who got their dick out for their best mate?

Nice. But Calum felt no shame. He could find no sense in the time he'd spent with Brix tonight, but he'd meant every kiss, every touch, and his heart told him Brix had too.

It didn't tell him what to do next, though. Calum had believed Brix when he'd said he wanted Calum—still believed him—but the defeat in Brix when he'd said they could never fuck had cut Calum to the bone.

Damn it. Calum banged his head on the tiles a final time before he shut off the shower and got out, padding naked across the landing.

His phone rang as he was drying off.

Lee.

Calum grabbed it and swiped the screen. "What time do you call this?"

"Half-seven. Why? Forgotten how clocks work?"

"Half-seven?" Calum ignored Lee's trademark sass and pulled his phone from his ear to check the time. "Fuck. Thought it was still the middle of the night."

"Looks like it too with those storm clouds lurking."

Calum glanced out of the window. Black cloud still hung heavy in the sky. "What are you doing up anyway? Are you okay?"

Lee laughed. "You've been up all night with Brix while the boat was out, and you're asking me if I'm okay? Dude, I slept like an orange-haired baby."

"So did I." Calum dropped his towel and snagged a T-shirt from the pile on the dresser. "Brix didn't."

"I'm not going to ask how you know that."

Mischief dripped from Lee's tone. Calum ignored it in favour of yanking some jeans up his legs. "Perhaps he told me, eh? Ever thought about that?"

"Nope. Sue me. How is he, anyway? Kim was wrecked when I saw him."

"When did you see Kim?"

"When I was getting out of my taxi."

"Your taxi?"

Lee sighed. "Yeah, numbnuts, my taxi. I stayed at my sister's last night, so I had to scarper before her kids woke up."

"Why?"

"Why do you think? So they don't start asking where Uncle Liam went."

Calum sank onto his bed. "Your sister makes you leave before her kids wake up so they won't find out you transitioned?"

"Actually, no. My sister's a stuck-up bitch, but she's not

that bad. It's me who can't handle it. My therapist reckons I'm scared they'll be disappointed by the new me."

"Are you?"

"Maybe. Can't be arsed to figure it out just yet, though, and anyway, I didn't call you to talk about my shit, so stop asking me Jeremy Kyle questions."

Calum grinned into a yawn. "Okay, okay . . . Brix's dad is fine, if that's what you wanted to know. Brix went to round him up from a pub in Porth Luck."

"Sounds about right. You sure you're okay? I can come over if you want? Keep you company till Brix gets back?"

Calum's smile died. "Why are you being nice?"

"I'm allowed."

"Not if there's some weird subtext you're not telling me about."

"Subtext? Whatever. I called cos Brix gets stressed about family shit and I wanted to check you weren't rocking in a corner, blaming yourself for any Lusmoore lunacy."

Lusmoore lunacy? Calum rubbed his eyes. "Brix isn't the crazy one in this house. He was worried, but who wouldn't be?"

"Me. I couldn't give two fucks if my dad drowned at sea."

"Understandable. We're not all the same."

"I know. You don't have to go big brother on me. I'm the one trying to be nice here, remember?"

"And you're good at it, but you'd be better if you just said what you want to say."

Silence. Then Lee let loose a sigh of her own. "I guess I'm trying to tell you not to freak out if Brix goes walkabout over the next few days. He's the nicest bloke in the world, but sometimes he needs space to figure out his own shit. Get away from all of ours."

Calum pictured Brix crouched on the cold ground, rain pelting him at the foot of the cliff, listening with more patience than anyone deserved to Calum's half-arsed explanation to why he'd run away from a fucking phone call. "You think I should give him some space?"

"Me?" Lee snorted. "What the fuck do I know? Say what I see, and I'm usually wrong."

"Can you do me a favour?"

"Providing it ain't sexual."

Calum rolled his eyes. "Can you get Lena to cancel my appointments today? I have to go somewhere."

"Sounds mysterious."

"Not really, but if I tell you where I'm going, I won't be able to change my mind."

"Is that likely?"

"Not sure yet. I'll let you know?"

Lee grunted. "Good enough for me. I'll sort your shit. Don't worry about anything, just keep in touch, yeah?"

"Will do. Thanks, squirt. I owe you."

"Doesn't work like that in Porth Ewan. Nice people are real, and you don't owe me jack."

Lee hung up, leaving Calum with burning eyes he couldn't explain, but he didn't dwell on it long. He pocketed his phone and keys, and went downstairs. Fed the cats. Checked on the chickens.

He scooped Bongo up. Before Porth Ewan, he'd had no idea that holding a chicken could be so relaxing, but as he stood in the damp early morning, counting Bongo's heartbeat and absorbing her quiet clucks, he reckoned only holding Brix would be better.

Brix.

The purpose of Calum's mission today returned full force.

He set Bongo down and went back inside, patting his jacket pocket for his wallet.

It wasn't there, or in the bowl of crap on the kitchen table.

Fuck's sake.

Calum jogged upstairs and checked his bedroom—grabbing his bag and a set of long-forgotten keys—and the bathroom, but he came up blank, which left only one place.

Venturing into Brix's room felt like returning to the scene of a well-meant crime. Gaze down, Calum retrieved his wallet from the floor by the bedside table, but the clear space above caught his attention. Something was missing. The washbag—it had gone—and in the silence of the empty cottage, its absence seemed more significant than Calum could explain.

He shoved the wallet in his pocket and fled the cottage. The bus stop was a five-minute walk along the seafront. On the way, Calum looked up each time a vehicle passed, expecting Brix's van to rumble past, but it didn't happen, and as the bus left Porth Ewan behind a while later, the pang in his heart was almost too much to bear.

Paddington Station was as hellish as Calum remembered. Worse. The smell, the crowds, and the cold draft that whistled around every corner, reminding him, as he left the station behind, how much he'd grown to despise city life. How much he despised *trains*, though that might've been because a tunnel had caused him to miss Brix's call, and he'd spent most of the journey worrying that Brix was angry that he'd cancelled his appointments.

If he even cares.

Calum knew he did. He *knew*. But being back in London made it all too easy for the self-doubt monster to consume him again, and the set of keys he'd shoved in his bag felt like a live grenade. A dread that intensified as the building that had once housed Black Star Ink loomed into view, and it became obvious that the studio was being converted into a café.

Shit. Calum's heart sank. He'd expected the shop to be stripped, but he'd been hanging onto the hope that Rob had left the sentimental things behind. The treasure that would be everyone else's trash.

Dottie.

Calum pinched his eyes. All this time, and now he was going to lose it in the street over an ancient tattoo machine.

"All right there, mate?"

Calum turned to the builder who'd called out. "Yeah, I used to work here. Just looking for some stuff. Seen any tattoo equipment lying around?"

"Tattoo equipment? You mean needles and shit?"

"An old machine. Not worth shit, so I'm hoping it got left behind."

The workman jumped down from his stepladder and hollered into the back of the shop. "Oi! Curly! Get out here."

A younger man appeared, covered in paint and dust. "What?"

"Him over there." The older dude pointed. "Used to work here. Says he's looking for some tattoo shit. What happened to that box we found in the office a few days ago?"

"It's in the skip, innit."

"Where's the skip?" Calum asked. There wasn't one outside.

"It's at our other site down the road," the first man said. "The barber's next to the Abbey National."

Calum frowned. *Abbey National?*

"He means Santander," Curly said. "Stev's stuck in the nineties. We've had the fucking Charlatans on repeat all day."

Stev responded with a cuff to Curly's ear.

Calum took advantage of their distraction and dashed away,

He jogged down the road. It didn't take long to spot the skip outside Santander, and he approached it with wary hope. He'd lied to the builders. Dottie was a vintage machine, worth more than three of some of the sleek new ones Brix had at Blood Rush, but—and it was a big but—as far as Calum knew,

Rob had no idea of her value, so there was a chance that he hadn't flogged her on eBay.

The skip was full, piled high with rubble and junk. Calum peered over the side, then caught the eye of a workman. "Stev and Curly sent me to look for something."

"Have at it, mate." The workman went back to his paper. "It's being collected tonight."

Calum climbed over the side of the skip and rummaged around, seizing any scrap of cardboard he came across in case it was the elusive box.

It wasn't. Not for the first seventy times. He'd about given up hope by the time his hands scraped the side of the battered Amazon box he'd once kept flash posters in.

Stomach in his mouth, he eased the box from beneath a pile of broken bricks. At the top, he found spare parts to the sterilising machine Rob must've taken, and then damaged packs of gloves and antiseptic. The hope in his chest faded—then *soared*, cos right at the bottom, was the scuffed tattoo gun he'd carried since his apprentice days.

Dottie.

Calum's heart leapt. She was in *so many* bits, but he'd found her, and now that she was safe in his arms, there was no reason for him to stay in London a minute longer.

He wrapped Dottie in his coat and scrambled out of the skip, ignoring the startled gaze of a nearby plumber. His phone buzzed as his feet hit the ground: a message . . . from Brix.

Fuck. Calum stared at the phone. With all the trepidation of returning to London, he hadn't forgotten to call Brix back, he just...hadn't done it. Choked by years old fears, he'd been too afraid, and even now—even knowing it was *Brix* behind the message—he still braced for a barrage of abuse.

Get out of the city.

Message unread, Calum pocketed the phone and ran for the station, perspective returning with every step he took in the right direction. Every step he took towards Brix. Their friendship was complicated. But real. *Brix* was real, and by the time Calum collapsed on a train seat and read the message lighting his phone screen, he was ready for the chain reaction it set off.

Brix: Pls come home. So much to tell u

Calum didn't doubt it, and as he replayed every moment he'd spent with Brix in Porth Ewan, pushing the magic of the sea aside, tiny pieces of a puzzle he'd never thought to look for slotted into place.

Oh, Brix.

Brix sat in the idling van, tracking the trickle of commuters who periodically emerged from Truro train station, ignoring the strongest urge he'd had to smoke in months. *Years.* An urge that kept his fingers busy tapping the dashboard, his knee, and anything else he touched.

"Take a minute. Calm yourself, boy. You're like a cat in heat."

"You shouldn't have gone out, Dad. Not at your age."

"That right? Well, if you'd bought me a few ales like you'd said you would, I'd have been too bloody drunk, eh?"

John Lusmoore's logic had made a sick kind of sense, but Brix found himself unable to heed the snark-hidden pearl of wisdom.

Take a minute. Calm yourself, lad.

Yeah, right.

Brix got out of the van and opened the back, nose-blind to the waft of stale chicken shit. He grabbed the roll of bin bags from the foot-well and gathered the newspapers and straw left over from the last rescue run, a job he should've done weeks ago, but it didn't take as long as he hoped. He dumped the bag in a nearby bin, and glanced north for the millionth time, searching for any sign of an incoming train. It didn't take a genius to figure out that Calum had gone back to London, a reality that made Brix sick to his stomach. *Should've been with him.* But hindsight was a wonderful thing. And while Brix regretted running out on Calum without telling him how much the night they'd spent together meant to him, he couldn't bring himself to regret anything else, even though what had passed between them could never happen again.

Despite his diligent vigil, a train pulled into the station on the London line without him noticing its approach. His heart flipped. *Calum's train.* It had to be. Calum's text had said he'd be home by ten, a prospect that, six hours ago, had seemed an unbearable wait. So why was Brix's heart in his throat now? When Calum was just a few minutes away?

Because you're about to tell him, on a scale of one to ten, how fucked up you really are.

"Brix?"

Brix jumped, as if he hadn't been expecting Calum to appear at any moment. "Hey."

Calum grinned a little, though his eyes were cautious. "Hey yourself. You all right?"

"Think so."

"Did you get some sleep?"

"Nope. You?"

"On the train. Don't worry about me. I'm fine."

And as Brix stared at Calum, he saw that he really was. Though wary, Calum's gaze was steady and strong, his half smile honest and true. He looked . . . lighter? Like a burden had slipped from his shoulders, despite the fact that he was carrying a mysterious bundle wrapped in his jacket.

Brix inclined his head towards it. "What you got there?"

"Dottie."

"Dottie?"

"My coil from Black Star. Found her in a skip down the road from the shop."

So he had been back to his old place. "Oh yeah? What else did you find?"

"Nothing that mattered. Rob was long gone, but I wasn't after him anyway. Just wanted Dottie safe."

"You look happy."

Calum shrugged. "I am. I feel free . . . at least as free as I can be while you're being so fucking vague."

From anyone else, Calum's statement would've seemed combative, but as Brix searched his face again, he found nothing but concern-laced curiosity, and his own heart broke a little more. "You think I'm a bit mental, eh?"

"No, I think there's something I don't know, because that's what you've told me, and I believe you."

Brix found no joy in Calum's acceptance of the truth, not yet. "Are you coming home?"

"Mate, I never left." Calum stepped forward when Brix didn't respond, and took his hand. "Wherever you need me, I'm there."

"Can we go for a drive?"

"*Whatever you need*, Brix."

Brix drove to the moors ten miles inland from Porth Ewan. Calum watched dark hills and fields slip by, and then cocked Brix a quizzical grin. "We're not going to the sea?"

"Not this time. I want to show you there's more to this place than getting wet."

"Fair enough." Calum went back to watching scenery he could barely see.

Brix missed his face.

"There's an old Porth Ewan rumour that my dad buried

my mum out there." He waited for Calum to look at him again and waved a hand at the expanse of flat ground. "Offed her and put her in the ground."

Calum snorted. "Your mum left twenty years ago. That's not old by Porth Ewan standards. Some old geezer was telling me about his uncle the other day. Took me ages to realise he was talking about a dude from the sixteenth century. You seafolk have no concept of time."

Brix couldn't argue with that. How often had his family torn themselves apart over a slight that had happened before any of them were born? "Despite all that, it's a good place really. Healing. I don't know what would've happened to me if I hadn't come back here."

"It is magic," Calum agreed as Brix pulled into a parking spot and shut off the engine. "But it didn't heal you completely, did it?"

"No."

Calum's gaze flickered to the moors and back again before he took a breath and seemed to steel himself. "I think I know what you're going to tell me."

"Doubt it."

"So did I when it came to me, but it makes sense. You've told me so much already. I can't think of much else you'd truly believe you had to hide."

Brix's pulse nosedived, vision narrowing, white spots dancing where Calum should've been. "I—"

No.

He couldn't do it.

"Brix."

No. He closed his eyes, shutting Calum out. *I can't.*

"You can." Calum wrapped his warm hands around Brix's ice-cold fingers. "You can tell me anything, even that, and I'll never turn away from you, I promise."

His promises were worth so much more than anyone else's.

Brix opened his eyes.

Calum's dark gaze was right there, a port in a storm, halfway to a hug while his arms stayed put.

Brix choked on the words. "I can't say it."

"You *can*."

Could he? Brix's heart stuttered again, like a steamroller backfiring in his chest. It hurt—*everything* hurt, except his fingers wrapped up in Calum's.

"I have HIV." Brix waited for Calum to rip his hands away. *Steeled* himself, as if he wouldn't shatter into a thousand pieces. "Did you fucking hear me?"

"I heard you." Calum moved *closer*, his voice soft and devoid of the disgust Brix had been so sure was heading his way, even from Calum.

Devoid of *shock*.

"You knew."

Not a question, but Calum nodded. "I had a lot of time to think on the train today. Otherwise, I might've figured it out quicker, and I'm so sorry about that. I'm sorry you had to go through this to tell me."

The apology washed over Brix, ringing in his ears as his brain set off at a million miles an hour again, nausea twisting his gut. If Calum had worked it out, who else had? Kim? Lee?

Dad.

Brix's stomach wrenched harder and for a protracted beat, he feared he truly would vomit.

"It's not obvious, if that's what you're worried about." Calum squeezed Brix's hands hard enough to bend the bones, anchoring him. "I think I'm the only person on earth so obsessed with you, and combined with the sex, the blood thing when I hurt myself, the pills you hide in your washbag...but I wasn't certain until you said it."

"And now you are." Brix's vision remained hazy. "Now you *know*."

"I do. And I'm glad of it. I'm just...fucking *furious* I didn't know years ago, cos my heart is killing me knowing you've been alone with this for so fucking long."

Again with the *fucks*. But Brix was too distracted by the fact Calum had worked out he'd never told *anyone* before this messy moment to make a joke of it. He stared out over the black moors, then closed his eyes as Calum pulled him into the embrace he'd needed so long ago, when life as he'd known it back then had come to a shattering end.

Calum held him forever, wrapping him in warmth, and a silence that healed some of the deepest cracks in Brix's heart.

Only the cold drove them apart, and Calum's soft kiss at Brix's cheek felt like goodbye.

Calum got out of the van.

Devastation hit Brix like a wrecking ball. Then bitter wind vanquished it as the van door beside him whipped open, gifting him a full frontal of Calum's lovely face.

Calum kissed him again, on the lips this time. "Shove over. I'm driving us home. We can talk more on the way, but it's okay if you need to drift."

Drift. How did Calum know Brix had been doing that his whole fucking life?

Brix scooted to the passenger seat as Calum claimed the space behind the wheel. "I didn't know you had a licence."

"Maybe I haven't." Calum turned the key. "You're just gonna have to trust me."

"I do trust you. You're my best friend . . . you always were."

Calum backed the van out of the space and spun around towards the road. "Some best friend. I wasn't there when you needed me most. You were in London when you found out, weren't you? That's why you came back here?"

"Yeah." Brix waited until Calum pulled onto the deserted road before he let out a sigh he'd been holding for a hundred years. "My dad found me the same state as I did you. Except I made it to Ladock bus station. I wasn't drunk, mind. Though he probably thought I was."

"Had you just found out?" Calum kept his eyes on the road, easing the van around the tight, Cornish corners. "I mean—been diagnosed—is that the right word?"

Brix shrugged. "I don't think it matters, but I'd known a few weeks by the time I crawled back here. Do you remember that ink convention in Croydon? When Two-Minute Tony won?"

"I heard about it, but I wasn't there."

"Really?" Brix sifted through memories that felt like they belonged to someone else. "You weren't there?"

"I was away. You were gone when I came back, and no one seemed to know where."

"I'm sorry."

Calum's hand left the steering wheel and touched Brix's, his fingertips tracing a burning trail across Brix's knuckles. "Don't be sorry. Just keep talking, eh? For as long as you need."

For as long as you need. Emotion warred with numbness. For now, numbness won out. "I've never told anyone . . . except Jordan."

Calum shot him another sideways glance. "Jordan?"

"I was supposed to exhibit at Croydon, but I woke up that morning feeling like shit, so I didn't go. Jordan went to work while I stayed in bed at his place. I thought it was just a hang-over or something, but when he got home, I had a headache so bad I was screaming."

Calum turned the van left, his expression inscrutable.

Brix took a deep breath and continued. "The hospital thought I had meningitis. They put me in an isolation ward and told Jordan to call my family. Luckily, he didn't know how, cos the next morning…"

"Go on," Calum urged. "You're okay."

I love him.

Brix shivered through that reality and forced the rest of it out. "They sedated me overnight so I could sleep, and the next morning, a different doctor came round. Said he was going to do some tests—he didn't say what, and I didn't ask. I was distracted, Jordan had disappeared, and he'd been gone ages, and I was so fucking ill and scared, I couldn't figure out why he'd left me."

"He knew, didn't he?"

"That obvious, eh?" Brix tipped his head back. Talking about this—with Calum—was easier than he'd expected, but the weight of keeping it to himself so long had left him drained. "Well, you're right. He scarpered, and that was the last I saw of him for a while. The doctor came back that after-noon with a nurse from the sexual health clinic. They told me I had a recent HIV infection that was probably what was making me so ill—it's called seroconversion, not everyone gets it—then they gave me a number to call when I was discharged and that was it."

"That was it?"

Brix shrugged. "They didn't boot me out, but there wasn't much they could do for me. I left as soon as I could walk."

"Where did you go?"

"To find Jordan."

Calum fell silent as the sea came into view. His eyes remained on the road, but Brix could tell his mind was racing, drawing the same conclusions Brix had all those years ago.

"Don't hurt your brain, Cal. Whatever you're thinking is probably true."

"You got it from Jordan?"

Brix eased his aching head into a slow nod. "He'd known for six months but done nothing about it. We didn't bareback much—we didn't even *fuck* that much—but you know what things were like back then, with the drink and weed and shit. Stuff . . . happened, and the axe fell on me."

"I'm so sorry."

Brix turned to Calum as the van eased to a stop outside the cottage. "Ain't your fault."

"It isn't yours either."

"Isn't it? I got tanked up and had unprotected sex—more than once—with someone I knew was sleeping around with half of Camden. You can't deny how fucking stupid that was."

"No more than you'll ever convince me you deserved this." Calum shut off the engine and exited the van, slamming the door.

Brix stared after him.

I told him.

It didn't seem real, but Calum's abrupt absence made his bones ache too much to linger in the cold van.

He got out and trailed Calum to the front door. "Are you angry with me?"

Calum kicked the door open. "Never. I'm just *angry*, Brix. None of this is fucking fair—to *you*. And you're sitting in front of me worrying about how this is gonna affect *me*. And don't try to deny it, or we really will fall out."

The only falling Brix was doing was *over*, as two days without sleep caught up with him.

He stumbled.

Calum caught him. "Bed. Now."

Brix didn't argue. Letting Calum lead him upstairs and sit him on the edge of his bed had begun to feel normal.

He bent to untie his boots.

Calum beat him to it and eased them off his feet.

Dude, you don't have to undress me.

But the words didn't find their way to Brix's tongue. Instead, he raised his arms so Calum could slip his T-shirt off, then forced himself to stand and swap his jeans for sweats.

Calum disappeared. Brix's heart followed him, but his body couldn't comply. He crawled into bed, so tired the room spun, even as he strained to hear any sign that Calum had come back. For too long, there was nothing, then the bed dipped behind him and Brix found his head in the soothing safety of Calum's lap.

"Will you tell me what it's like?"

Brix opened his eyes. "What it's like?"

"Living with it." Calum stared down. "Does it make you sick?"

"Not often. Most days I forget I have it."

Calum's gaze turned quizzical. "I don't get that."

Brix relinquished the best pillow in the world and sat up, rotating so his legs could wrap around Calum's waist, a move that seemed to surprise Calum, until Brix took his hands. "It doesn't make me ill. I've been on the medication for years now. My viral load is undetectable, and my CD4 count is strong. Honestly, the meds give me more trouble than the disease."

"...Truvada?"

A few years ago, Brix would've been surprised Calum had

heard of the magic blue pill that kept him alive, but times were changing fast. "At the moment, but the clinic switches it up sometimes. Right now, I take Truvada combined with another drug. Three fat pills a day, two red, one blue."

"And the side effects are nasty?"

"Only if I don't pay attention. You gotta take them regularly, with food, and leave off the binge drinking and shit. That blue pill's a bitch on an empty stomach. Hurts like hell and gives me vertigo."

"That's why you get dizzy sometimes?"

"You've noticed, eh? Thought I was better at hiding it than that."

Calum tucked a lock of Brix's wild hair behind his ear. "Most people don't stare at you as much as I do, remember?"

"You can stare at me all you like."

"Noted." Calum's grin was dazzling. Then it faded. "What else do the meds do? You've seemed really tired since I came here. Is that connected, or is there something else?"

"I think it's my head." Brix tapped his temple. "*Life* makes me tired, you know? As far as the rest of it, I just try to look at the numbers and go from there."

"Your blood count? The CD4 and stuff? I think I know what it all means, but I've never looked at it this hard."

"Why would you? Don't look so fucking guilty."

Calum scrubbed a hand over his beard. "I'll stop feeling guilty when I understand what it all means for you. Humour me, yeah?"

"All right." Brix delved into the knowledge he'd never dreamed he'd have. "Because the meds work for me, my viral load is undetectable—which means I have fuck-all active HIV in my blood. And my CD4 count is high, normal, like yours probably, which means my immune system is healthy."

"Healthy. That's a good place to be."

"I know. I'm lucky that my biggest battle is with myself, and it might've been that way even without this happening to me."

"What do you mean?"

Brix traced an abstract pattern on Calum's wrist. "It just seems too good to be true sometimes, you know? Like I'm building a house of cards and it's gonna blow down every time I get a fucking cold. Makes me want it over with. To let it kill me now so I don't have to fight it."

"But you're not ill and it's not going to kill you."

"I know . . . and I believe it most days, but it gets on top of me when other shit gets in my head."

"Because you were prone to depression before?"

When you tried to off yourself. Brix heard the end of Calum's unspoken sentence loud and clear. "You sound like my nurse. She reckons HIV probably saved me. I thought she was off her tits when she first said it, but it makes more sense these days. I was on self-destruct in London, but I'd never have come back here if things hadn't gone so wrong with Jordan, and who knows what mess I'd be in now."

Calum smiled. "I thought all Porth Ewan folk came home eventually."

"Not alive, they don't. It's the sea. We need it, it's who we are, and I wouldn't have survived this without it."

"You're not going to survive the night if you don't get some sleep." Calum touched Brix's face, rubbing the pad of his thumbs over Brix's stinging eyelids. "We can talk forever, if that's what you need, but it'll all still be here tomorrow."

"Will you?"

"Me?"

Brix leaned into Calum's touch. "Will you be here tomorrow . . . I mean, right here? With me?"

"If that's what you want."

"I want you to stay." *Forever*. But fatigue finally won the war and Brix ran out of words, and everything else he needed to hold himself up.

Calum eased him down and onto his side, moulding his bigger frame behind Brix, arms around him, chin on his head. "Then I'll stay."

A strangled sound—a sob, maybe— snarled in Brix's chest.

"Shh." Calum kissed his neck. "Sleep, mate. I'm here."

CHAPTER
EIGHTEEN

Calum studied the hole in the chicken wire. It looked like a hen had tried to dig out of the enclosure, but as far as he could tell, they were all still inside.

He counted heads to be sure. Lost track as they wandered in and out, laying their morning eggs, screeching at him to go away. Even Bongo. Who knew chickens liked their privacy so much?

Calum did *now*.

He stepped away, still pondering the hole in the fence.

Foxes? Wolves?

Bears?

His city stripes were starting to show. And actually, it didn't matter. There was a hole and it needed to be fixed, and there was no way Calum was waking Brix to ask him for a hammer.

He moved to the shed and rummaged among the animal feed and tools, trying not to glance up at the bedroom window. The urge to check on Brix was strong, but he'd been dead asleep when Calum had left him, and he needed to stay that way, for a few more hours at least.

He's okay. Calum took a breath, mind still racing as he armed himself with a hammer and a box of nails. While Brix had slept, Google had been his best friend, filling in a few blanks they hadn't got to yesterday—medication, long-term prognosis.

Sex.

Cos that's what matters?

It wasn't, but facts kept Calum calm, and he'd inhaled enough of them this morning to run a sexual health clinic. Enough of them to *know* that if Brix's viral load was undetectable, they could have *unprotected* sex and still be safe.

Stop thinking about sex.

Calum focused on the hole in the fence. He'd just about fudged it when a battered Defender drove down the side of the cottage and pulled up by the gate.

John Lusmoore. Calum didn't know how he knew, just that he did. He had no clue who his female companion was, though. Or if they had a clue who he was.

He locked the shed and moved to the gate, hand on the bolt to let them through. But they stopped a few feet away, staring, their curiosity as obvious as Calum's.

Their *suspicion*, if the harsh glare Brix's dad sent his way was anything to go by. "You that London fella?"

"Calum."

"That was the name," the woman said. "Got all the girls in town all aflutter, he has, John."

John grunted. "A carthorse gets those twits excited. Where's my boy at? Workin'? We didn't see him at the shop."

"He's asleep." Calum inclined his head at the cottage. "Knackered from the last few days."

"See?" The woman elbowed John's ribs. "Told you jumping

on that boat at all hours was going to upset him. I'm Peg, by the way. The prodigal son's favourite aunt."

Favourite aunt bore little resemblance to the Aunt Peg Brix had described, but Calum couldn't help warming to her. She had Brix's smile, and Calum had been under its spell for as long as he could remember. "Do you want me to wake him?"

"Too late."

Brix's smoky voice startled Calum. He turned to find Brix behind him, rumpled, gorgeous, and a million times better than he'd looked twelve hours ago.

Eyes bright, they stared at each other, a thousand things to say, but no words to say them.

John cleared his throat. "What you been doing with that chook fence, boy? Looks like you drove the van over it."

Brix blinked. "Hmm?"

"That bloody mess." John pointed. "It's all over the place."

Calum winced. "There was a hole when I got up—that's my shit attempt at fixing it."

Unimpressed, John's glower deepened. Brix peered beyond them to see what all the fuss was about, then turned to Calum with a smile that was *kind*. "It ain't bad."

Calum didn't believe that any more than the clutch of extra Lusmoores crowding the gate.

He stepped back as John and Peg pushed their way through.

"Come on." John pointed again. "You need to move the fence post for starters. I'll show you."

He strode across the garden without waiting to see if Calum followed.

Lacking any better ideas, Calum trailed after him and joined him at the fence, blocking out Peg's cackle of laughter.

"I was worried about foxes." And bears, but he kept that to himself. "Sorry if I fucked it up."

John stooped, frowning at the tragedy Calum and his borrowed hammer had left behind. "Don't be sorry, lad. It was better than leaving it open. Hundreds of foxes round here, even this close to the sea. And they won't take one gal, they'll take them all. Right bastards, they are."

"You think a fox made the hole?"

"Not likely. They don't leave none alive when they get in. You've lost a few nails in the storm. See 'ere?" John pointed to more holes in the nearest post, unlocking Calum's wayward work as he went, replacing it with his own. "Do you right, boy, it ain't as bad as I thought. I can see where you were goin', and it might've worked if you'd secured the post properly."

Calum crouched, studying the gaping chasm between his skill level and John's. "Nice of you to say, but securing the post never occurred to me."

John laughed, a deep rumbling chuckle that eclipsed his surly demeanour. "Jesus-wept. Your face. I'm not telling you ya killed a dog or summit. You think that boy in there built this thing on his own? No, these bare hands did all the bloody work while he heckled me from that bench over there."

"That doesn't sound like Brix."

John shrugged. "Well . . . he mighta hammered in a few nails when I told 'im to. Ain't none of us born knowing how to build the ark."

The obtuse biblical reference caught Calum off guard, but John wasn't looking at him. Calum followed his gaze to the kitchen window, where he could just about make out Brix and Peg sitting at the table.

"He looks like Peg," Calum mused to himself as much as John.

John grunted. "Sounds like her too, without the gob on him, though. Abel's like his mum, pretty and daft."

"Do you miss them?"

"Miss 'em?" John hammered another nail into the post. "I miss my baby gal, and the boy maybe—both of 'em, actually, when him in there goes off on one—but their ma can fall in the sea for all I care, if the sea weren't too good for the likes of her."

The brutal sentiment was softened by a gleam in John's eyes that Calum had seen in Brix. Perhaps they were more alike than anyone knew. "Is the fence safe now?"

"It'll do. Help an old man up, will ya?"

Calum rose and helped John to his feet. He turned up the path, but John's hand on his arm stayed him.

"What you doin' down here anyway? It's been a few months now, eh? You sticking around?"

Twenty-four hours ago, Calum would've second guessed his answer. Now, he didn't blink. "I'm sticking around."

His certainty earned him another Lusmoore grunt as John let go of his arm to clap a heavy palm to his back. "That'll do me. I think the boy likes your company, and he's a good lad. Deserves to be 'appy, so don't fuck it up."

"I—"

John was already walking away.

It was gone five by the time Peg ran out of steam. By then, Calum was a little in love with her, and he was daft enough to tell Brix.

"Fucking hell." Brix shook with laughter. "You really have

been Lusmoored if you think that woman's *sweet*. She's an arsehole."

"You love her, though."

"I love them all. Don't make them sweet, it makes them family . . . a family of arseholes."

"Have you ever thought about telling them?"

"That they're arseholes? I tell them all the time."

Calum waited for Brix to realise his deflection hadn't worked.

It didn't take long. A beat passed, and Brix sighed, turning away to mess with the kettle. "I could never tell them. It was their biggest fear when I came out, and I promised them it would never happen."

Calum had no sensible answer to that. He let it go and retreated to the living room while Brix did whatever he trying to do with the kettle. It wasn't raining, but the sky was dark. Heavy. And it seemed fitting for the mood fast descending on Calum. Sex invaded his brain again, and shoving it aside was a bridge to far.

He let his thoughts run free, returning to the googling he'd done while Brix had slept. If it was accurate, Brix's fear of intimacy was illogical, but when had fear ever made sense? Which led him to the barbed notion that perhaps he didn't want to fuck Calum regardless. And then the realisation that the thought of Brix never sharing that closeness with *anyone* ever again hurt worse than anything.

"Where did you go?" Brix was suddenly in front of Calum, standing so close Calum's skin tingled and his hands itched to touch him, but Brix got there first. He tapped Calum's temple. "I don't like it when you disappear on me. What are you thinking about?"

Tell him the truth. "I'm thinking about sex."

"Oh." The shift in Brix was instant. He stepped away, his hands dropping to his sides. "Wondering about where you can get some?"

"Don't."

"Sorry." Brix backed slowly to a nearby chair and sat down. "I just—I don't know how to talk about sex anymore."

Yes, you do. Calum tried not to picture how Brix's hands had felt on his dick. Fought to bring himself back to the science he'd learned by heart in the misty light of a Porth Ewan early morning. "I don't get it."

"Get what?"

"I don't get why you said you'll never have sex again."

Brix didn't blink. "Seriously? Out of everything, that's what you need explaining to you?"

"I'm trying to understand. Your status is undetectable, but—"

"But what?" Brix snapped.

"You're not infectious." Calum inched through the minefield. "If you bag up, there's no reason you can't have all the sex in the world."

"Ah . . . you've been googling, eh?"

"Wouldn't you?"

"I *did*, like a fucking lunatic, when I thought being positive meant I couldn't ink anymore. I know how it works."

"So why can't you have sex? With anyone, not just me."

"Because I'm fucking scared of it!" The shout burst free from Brix's chest like he'd wrenched it from the earth's core. It didn't shock Calum. He'd seen it building. But it seemed to shock Brix and he slapped a hand over his mouth, as if he could shove the words back in.

Easy.

Take a breath.

Calum manifested the words he couldn't speak and waited.

Brix let his hand drop. "It's like how I was scared of putting a needle to someone, but this is worse . . . much worse, especially if we're talking about me and you."

"Me and you?"

"Don't look so shocked. You just said it."

"I know, but hearing it from you blows my mind." Calum braved a step forward. "Are you worried about a condom breaking? Cos all that googling told me that whoever you were with wouldn't even need the emergency meds as long as you're undetectable. And there's PrEP—what?"

Brix shook his head. "Preventive PrEP isn't available on the NHS. They only give it out if you've had a high-risk exposure. And I would *die* before I let you spend a fortune on medication you don't need when you're fucking healthy without it."

"So no PrEP then. Fuck me without it. Fuck *whoever* without it." Calum nudged Brix's legs apart and crouched down, dropping his palms on Brix's thighs. *He's shaking.* "I'm not telling you how to feel, but don't shut yourself off. It's not fair, you don't deserve it."

"Being unfair don't change shit."

Brix's jaw remained set, but his hands crept towards Calum's. Unconscious, maybe, but Calum took heart in it and claimed Brix's fingers. "How did you get past this fear with tattooing?"

"I didn't for the first six months I was back here. Didn't have it in me. I was still sick as a dog, too. Could hardly get up some days."

"What changed?"

"The sea, maybe?" Brix shrugged. "Summer faded and the storms came. I don't like the cold, but watching the waves batter the rocks was good for my soul . . . cleansing, I guess. In the end, I made a deal with my HIV counsellor that I'd set up Blood Rush anyway, give the cool folks I knew a place to work, then at least try to start inking again . . . and keep inking, over and over, until I'd convinced myself I wasn't gonna kill anyone."

"Your counsellor sounds pretty wise."

"She was."

"Was?"

"I only had her for six months. After that, I was on my own —apart from the clinic, but I only see them every six months now."

Twice a year. For a disease that would haunt Brix for the rest of his life. Calum drew a random design on Brix's clothed thigh. "Her theory worked though, didn't it? You did more ink the other day than I've done all week."

"It's not the same as sticking my dick in someone."

"Isn't it?"

"No—listen, fuck—Calum, *God*." Brix clenched his eyes shut and scrubbed at them, then refocused with a biblical sigh. "I know it's irrational . . . I *know*, but I can't be the reason someone feels like I do now. I can live with everything else, but not that, Cal. I can't do it."

Calum sighed too, defeat washing over him. "For what it's worth, I want you to know that you deserve all the love in the world, and there's no reason outside of your own head that you can't have it, but I hear you. And I'm *here* for you, okay? Whatever happens."

Brix nodded, already zoning out, needing the space Lee had warned Calum about.

Let him breathe. Calum rose, but as he turned towards the stairs, there was one last question he had to ask. "What happened between you and Jordan when you found him? You never told me."

Brix's troubled gaze flashed, guilt blazing, hot and sharp. "I hit him . . . a lot, like the Lusmoore I am. Ironic, eh? The only time I toe the family line and they'll never know."

"You beat him up?"

"Yup."

Calum had no answer to that either. He left Brix to his brooding and went upstairs to change out of the clothes he'd worn to muck about in the chicken run. He undressed and went to the window, opening it wide, letting the bitter wind cut into his bare skin. With Brix's faith in the sea echoing in his mind, he waited for it to ease the pain in his heart. But nothing happened, save a tingling rush of goose bumps, and despair swamped him again.

He shut the window and sank onto his bed. The last few days had left him numb, and the weight of all Brix had shared was only now sinking in. A ripple in the pond. His soul ached for Brix and all he'd survived, but more than that, the fact that he'd been alone, while Calum had wasted four years with Rob . . .

Jesus.

Calum couldn't take it. He inhaled a deep, shuddering breath.

Then he put his head in his hands and cried.

The dark outline of the rose seemed to Brix to ink itself, like he'd etched the design a thousand times over, which wasn't as fanciful as it seemed. In fifteen years of tattooing, he'd seen more than his fair share of roses, even big ones like this—a huge, intricate collection of vintage blooms, splayed across the back of the burlesque dancer occupying his table.

Taz. Combined with the ink she already had, it was going to look awesome. At least, it would if he ever got it finished. Taz had a rowdy stomach. She rarely lasted an hour under the needle before she tapped out and ran for the bathroom.

Forty minutes in, Brix changed his needle and switched from outlining to the first layer of shading, blending the gradient. Trying not to notice Calum moving through the studio to hang out with Lee, like he always did when he was at a loose end.

They're good for each other. Maybe Lee had needed Calum as much as Brix had.

Need.

Brix's brain did a sharp one-eighty, leaving Lee far behind

as it nose-dived into the gutter . . . to his bed, where he'd spent the last ten nights sleeping with Calum stretched out beside him, neither one of them mentioning the giant elephant sharing their space. His hand shook, a minute tremor that was gone as suddenly as it had arrived, but it was intense enough for him to inhale and withdraw his gun from Taz's skin.

Calum looked up as Brix sat back, as though he'd heard Brix's racing thoughts. Their eyes met, and Calum grinned. Brix swallowed hard and returned the gesture, but his gut flipped, like it had every moment he had time to consider the hole Calum had kicked in his self-imposed wall of celibacy.

. . . there's no reason outside of your own head . . .

Calum wasn't wrong, but that wall...it was high, and made of the thickest stone. There was no way through, but fantasising about what could happen if Brix ever did was enough to make him sweat.

His time with Taz was running out. Brix wiped his brow and refocused. In his peripheral, Calum and Lee left. Brix panicked, but it was brief.

You sent them out, remember?

To get booze for Lena's party—

Taz tapped his leg. "Let me up."

"Whoa. Hang on." Brix took his foot from the pedal and pushed his stool back, holding the gun safely out of the way. "Okay, you're clear. Do what you gotta do."

Taz scrambled from the bench and dashed to the bathroom. Brix waited a few minutes, but when she didn't return, he knew they were done for the day.

He packed up and went to the desk to process the card Taz had left him. A simple task, but the computer frazzled him.

"Don't look at me." Lena slunk away. "You've got to learn."

"Why? Can't we be a cash business?"

"Only if you want every crook and dodgy biker round here using your business to wash their money."

"Thought you liked bikers."

"I like fucking them."

Did not need to know that, girl. "How do I key the amount in?"

Lena pursed her lips, stubborn until she realised Brix really didn't know. "Fuck's sake, move over."

She processed the payment in record time and printed the receipt. "She was in for one-eight-five."

But Brix was already distracted by the bundle Calum had brought home from London and transplanted into a box. It was tucked beneath an equipment locker, and Brix walked away while Lena was still talking.

He dug the box out and opened it. Inside, he found Dottie, the vintage machine Calum had trekked all the way to London to rescue.

She was in a dozen pieces, waiting for someone to bring her back to life, and Brix felt that to his fucking marrow.

He took the box to the break room and laid the parts out on the table. Even fragmented, Dottie was beautiful, and working on her happened without Brix making a conscious decision to do it.

She had a weak connector.

He went to the storeroom and searched boxes of mismatched machine parts until he found the washers and clip chord for his own long-lost coil machine.

The fix worked, and he was road-testing his handiwork when Kim stuck his head around the door a little while later, leaning casually on the architrave in a way that would've fooled anyone except Brix and Lena. "What's wrong?"

"Wrong? Nothing. All good in this hood."

"Yeah?" Brix turned down the power, checking Dottie's capability at a lower voltage. "Not freaking out over Lena going back to Bristol, then?"

"You're asking me now? When she's leaving on Sunday?"

Shit. Brix switched Dottie off. With his own bullshit to drown in, he'd neglected Kim, a friend as dear to him as Calum. "Sorry, mate. I'm so fucking self-absorbed at the moment."

Kim came closer, studying Dottie. "Brix, you don't know how to be selfish. But even if you did, it's okay. *I'm* okay. I love Lena to death, and that ain't gonna change."

Brix nodded slowly. "You deserve to be happy."

"Take your own advice, bud. Stop Lusmooring Calum."

"Fuck off."

"Yeah, yeah."

Kim fucked off and Brix didn't watch him go. They'd been friends a long time—they didn't have to say a lot to hear each other speak.

Stop Lusmooring Calum. Was that what he was doing? Being a stubborn *wanker* because he'd forgotten how to be anything else?

I want him.

Brix couldn't deny that, despite years of abstinence convincing him that he didn't even like sex. That he never had. A cage around his heart that had held until Calum had rocked up at Truro station with his gentle eyes and battered soul, lighting a flame in Brix that he couldn't smother.

I want him.

Brix returned to Dottie and tightened the last few remaining parts. Then he took a cloth to her and polished her within an inch of her life, wrapping her in an old shirt and returning her to Calum's station.

A sketchbook lay idle on the desk. Brix tore out a page and scrawled a note.

Meet me at the cave xx

"You know we don't get taught how to climb cliffs in Reading, right?"

Calum ducked into the cave, his cheeks flushed, mist droplets clinging to his dark hair. Despite his obvious bemusement, he was more beautiful than ever, and it was all Brix could do not to jump on him, tumble him to the dusty cave floor, and forgo all he had to say before they could leave their demons behind.

He settled for a nervous smile. "Good job you learned in Porth Ewan, then, eh?"

"I have Porth Ewan to thank for a lot of things."

"Me too." Brix grabbed Calum's hand, yanking him further inside. "Did you find Dottie?"

"Find her?" Calum stumbled into Brix's side before he steadied himself on a nearby crate. "I fucking fell on her like a long-lost lover."

His word choice fluttered Brix's pulse. He drowned in the heat of Calum's palm tucked against his. "I should've fixed her when you brought her home. I could see how special she was to you."

"She's more than special. I got her at Dalston junk market the day I got my apprenticeship. It's, uh, the same day I met you." Calum's shy smile peeked at Brix in the dark. "You gonna tell me why you've summoned me up here?"

"I'm gonna try. Sit with me?"

"Always."

Brix steered Calum to a clear corner of the cave where he and Abel had often hung out when they should've been at school. "Do you mean that?"

Calum eyed him. "That I'll always sit with you? Whenever you need me to? Yeah, Brix, I do."

"What if things go wrong?"

"With what?" Calum frowned. "Are we talking about sex? Cos I thought we'd covered that."

"I'm not talking about sex. I meant in general. I'm undetectable now, but that might not last if I become resistant to the meds, or liver-toxic, or my—fuck. No. That's not what I'm trying to say." Brix searched for the words to explain, but as ever, they weren't there when he needed them most.

Calum did that thing where he tucked Brix's hair behind his ears and rubbed his thumbs over his cheekbones, fingers grazing his jaw. "You have every chance of living as long as you might've done without HIV—longer, probably, seeing as you don't live like a heathen anymore. So that's what I'm going with until the universe gives me a reason not to. But whatever happens, I need you to know that the days of you facing this alone are over."

"I can't—" Brix took a breath and tried again. "I shouldn't ask that of you. And you can't ever stay because you feel sorry for me. Promise me you won't."

Calum blinked. "I don't feel sorry for you, Brix. I love you."

"Why?"

It wasn't the response Brix's heart screamed, and Calum seemed to know it. He smiled again, affection—*love*—blazing from his dark stare. "Because you're the strongest, kindest motherfucker I've ever known, and you make me feel ten feet tall."

"You know I love you too, don't you?"

Calum shrugged. "Some days. Others I find it so fucking hard to believe you'd even want to, but I'm working on that."

"I can help."

"You already do. I felt like a different man when I went back to London. A man who never would've let Rob shit all over him, and the only reason I didn't go and fucking tell him to sit on a thorny buttplug was you."

Brix grinned. "Me?"

"Who needs closure on bullshit that was never real when I can sit in a damp cave right here, right now?"

Tension bled out of Brix, loosening every muscle. He sat back, letting his head knock the stone behind him. "I didn't drag you up here to convince you that I love you. That'll happen on its own."

"So this *is* about sex?"

Brix rotated, stretching his legs over Calum's thighs, anchoring himself in how Calum's hands felt as they found their way to his calves. "There's some shit I need to say."

"I'm listening."

"Shit I should've said before I fed you scrumpy and kissed you."

"Still listening, Brix."

"I'm never going to fuck you without a condom."

Calum's lips twitched. "That's progress from never fucking me at all."

"I mean it."

"I believe you."

"And what if I can't ever do it at all? What if my dick's turned to ash?"

"Doubt it, mate. Felt pretty solid to me."

Heat flooded Brix's veins. His bones. His blood. "I'm serious. Thinking about it gives me palpitations. The bad kind."

"Come here." Calum coaxed him closer, until Brix had a knee either side of him, their faces inches apart. "Lee told me she had panic attacks when she first came here. Couldn't get on a bus by herself. She said you helped her get over it. What did you do?"

"Got on the bus with her twice a day for a month. Sixty trips to fucking *Bodmin*."

"Then what?"

"I followed the bus in the van so she could get off anytime she wanted. Sounds mad now."

"So why did you do it?"

"Because she deserved better than to be afraid of something so ordinary."

"Right." Calum nuzzled Brix's neck. "And you helped her get over that. I know it's not the same, but you deserve ordinary things too."

"Cal, us fucking isn't going to be ordinary."

"No?"

"*No.*" Brix claimed Calum's mouth, a kiss that started like all the others had—soft and sweet. Cautious. But there was nothing careful about the rawness that surged in him as they collided harder than they ever had before.

The roughness of his hands on Calum's skin.

The clash of teeth as the kiss deepened.

Brix pushed Calum against the cold stone, and the wall he'd built between them came tumbling down, leaving bright light in its wake. Sharper sensations. Everything, just...*more.*

"Fuck." Calum broke away, chest heaving, fighting for air. "Jesus."

Brix kissed him again. Then laughed, easing back as his pulse slowed. "Guess it's gonna be like breaking a dam?"

Calum rubbed his lips. "Feels that way. What's the opposite of ordinary?"

Brix kissed him again, losing his breath. Stealing Calum's. "*You.*"

Calum moved through the crowded room, feeling the heat of too many bodies packed into the Sea Bell for Lena's leaving do. Most faces he knew. Some he didn't, but he didn't mind. It didn't feel like one of Rob's seedy parties. Nothing in Porth Ewan ever did.

He found Kim and dropped onto the couch beside him. "Holding up?"

Kim waved his apple juice. "Living the dream."

"Are you driving later?"

"Someone's gotta her take to Bristol."

"Long goodbye?"

"Never goodbye." Kim smiled, love and affection warming his face before he sobered a little. "I took another call for you the other day. Been meaning to tell you."

"Again?" The beer in Calum's belly turned to acid. "What did he want?"

"Didn't ask. Just told him to die in a fire before I hopped on a train and skinned him alive."

"What?"

Kim shrugged like it was nothing. "Someone had to. Better me than Brix, cos he loves you enough to actually do it."

"You don't?"

"If you want me to love you like Brix does, you'll have to convince him to share." Kim winked, joking.

Calum relaxed. "Thanks for dealing with that. I could tell him to fuck off myself, but you've probably saved me another six months of harassment."

"Nah, we'd kill him first. Or hire Lena's dodgy mates to do it for us."

That didn't sound like a joke. Calum shook it off and enjoyed Kim's company a little while longer before Lee tracked him down and trod on his foot.

"I need you."

"For what? I already drove you to Bude this morning."

"I can't need you for more than one thing?"

"Depends what it is."

"Help me carry Lena's present in."

"She said she didn't want one," Kim countered.

Lee sent him a withering glare. "Didn't stop you building her a special box to cart her bass around in, did it?"

"I had extra pallets."

"You're extra, all right." Lee poked her tongue out and offered Calum her hand. "Please?"

Calum let her yank him up and followed her out into a car park crammed with motorbikes and leather-clad men with more ink than Brix.

Rubi was among them. He caught Calum's gaze and waved.

Calum waved back, but Lee crushed his toes again. "Jesus. *What?*"

"I don't really need your help. We got her a charm bracelet."

"Then why am I here?"

"Brix came out here. I thought you might want to go after him."

She wasn't wrong. Calum left her with a couple of bikers she seemed to know and abandoned the pub, following the call of the ocean. To Brix and the glow they'd cocooned around themselves since that explosive kiss in the caves.

And every kiss that had followed. Every touch. Every night they'd spent in Brix's bed, accepting their demons instead of fighting them.

"Waiting for a bus?"

Calum spun around. Brix stood behind him, smirking enough to turn Calum's brain to mush. "You fucker. I was looking for you."

"Up the road? I was six feet away from you five minutes ago. Where the fuck did you think I'd gone?"

"Lee said you came out here. She, uh, I don't know. It kinda sounded like you needed me."

Brix stepped closer. "I do need you."

"Oh yeah? For what?"

"Lots of things." Brix sidled into Calum's waiting arms. A perfect fit. Of course. "Keeping my chooks in order, managing Lee, setting that computer on fire. Most of all, though..." He brought his lips an inch from Calum's. "Most of all, for this."

Brix kissed Calum as if they were at home, shut away from the world, not standing at the side of the road for the whole of Porth Ewan to see. For his dad to see. The Blood Rush staff. He kissed Calum like he had no intention of ever stopping, and despite their public location, smouldering desire seared Calum's nerves.

He steadied himself on the drystone wall behind him. Brix pressed closer, *harder*, and Calum couldn't contain a low moan. "Are you trying to kill me?"

Brix's chest expanded with a shaky breath. "I don't know what I'm trying to do. I just saw you and this happened."

Calum searched his gaze. They'd talked about sex a lot since the cave, but he hadn't got a vibe that Brix was anywhere near ready to do anything about it. Had something shifted that he hadn't seen? Did the heat of Brix's *thick* cock digging into his thigh mean something?

Stop second-guessing him. But that was as impossible as not shifting to trace the length of Brix with his palm, shielding Brix from prying eyes with his body, revelling in Brix's snatched, hot breath, before he caught himself. "Fuck. Sorry."

Brix made a strangled sound.

Calum cupped his neck, fingers dancing on the bare skin of his throat. "Brix?"

"Yeah?"

"Are you okay?"

Brix nodded, *slowly*, wrapping his hands around Calum's wrists. "I was just thinking . . ."

"Thinking what?"

"That we need to leave. *Now*."

. . . we need to leave. Now.

Five words had never excited or terrified Calum so much. He let Brix lead him back inside to say goodbye to Lena. Then they left, and walking home felt like a dream.

A short dream, punctuated by heated stares and the loaded brush of Brix's fingers to his knuckles. The tenuous promise that what was to come could erase years of pain and heartache.

The cottage was dark. Zelda's amber eyes gleamed like smouldering embers, Dennis waiting in her shadow.

Calum fed them on autopilot. Washed his hands in the sink.

Brix slid his arms around his waist from behind and pressed his lips to his neck. "It's not a dream."

Calum gripped the counter, closing his eyes to Brix's touch. "How did you know I was wondering?"

"You always wonder. It's what makes you so fucking special."

Brix spun Calum around and kissed him like he had outside the pub, moulding his chest to Calum's, claiming his mouth. But the rest of it was different—his roaming hands, and the cant of his hips. The deeper press of his hard cock against Calum's.

The spark hit sun-dried tinder. Calum surged into the embrace and propelled Brix backward. They hit the table, the scrape of wood on tile a startling screech. But it had nothing on the rapid acceleration of Calum's heart. On the *throb* in his jeans.

He steadied them, snatching a breath. Then he kissed Brix again, bruising—*searching*—and he found the answer in Brix's blazing stare.

"Cal, I need you in my bed."

They stumbled to the stairs, leaving clothes on every step. Tumbled into Brix's room and fell on the bed.

Calum was naked.

Brix wasn't.

Calum pushed his jeans over his slim hips, underwear along for the ride, giving Brix every opportunity to stop him, but it didn't happen. Brix kicked the last of his clothes away and covered Calum's body with his own, skin to skin.

Heart to heart.

Calum felt Brix's pulse hammering in time with his own. "We can stop," he whispered. "Any fucking time, and it'll always be okay."

"I love you." Brix slid his hand along Calum's jaw. Then he moved like a snake, *lifting* Calum up the bed with a strength that belied his slender arms, and something clicked—exploded —and every doubt and fear faded a little bit more.

Brix's body was beautiful. Inked and lean. Calum couldn't get enough. He explored every inch, tipping Brix onto his back, gripping his thighs as he nuzzled his groin. "Can I blow you?"

"You don't have to do that."

"I want to. It won't hurt me, Brix. Let me do this for you."

Brix lay back, folding his hands behind his head. Calum took his cue and lowered his mouth to Brix's cock, sliding his lips over the tip, swallowing him whole with a long, slow slide.

"*Fuuuuuck.*" Brix jolted. "Boy, don't kill me before I bang you. I'll haunt you, I fucking swear."

A laugh knotted in Calum's chest, but the scent and taste of Brix distracted him. *Consumed* him. And not even Rob's evil voice could stop him making the most of Brix's every tremble and groan.

Nothing could. Bringing Brix to the edge was everything. Calum's blood zipped and his heart raced, as into this as he was to Brix touching him.

I'd swallow his cum.

Knowing Brix would never let him was a shadow on the horizon for another day.

Brix tugged him up and flipped them, wedging himself between Calum's legs, long fingers wrapping around Calum's dick. "You're so hard."

"You have that effect on me."

Brix laughed, but it was tinged with nerves. "I need you to get the lube and condoms I put in the drawer yesterday. I can't fucking do it."

Calum's eyes were heavy with arousal. Anticipation hazing his brain. But for Brix, anything. He kept his gaze locked on Brix and stretched an arm over his head, fumbling for the drawer. He didn't ask what had compelled Brix to gather supplies. Didn't look if there were three condoms in the box or thirty. Just grabbed one and the lube bottle and dropped them on the bed.

He shut the drawer for no reason whatsoever.

Again, Brix laughed. "Scared they'll jump back in?"

"Right now?" Calum traced Brix's lips with his tongue. "I'm not scared of anything."

"You should be. I feel like I've never done this before."

Of all the things Calum could fear in this moment, Brix being shit at sex wasn't one of them. The look in his eye, though…it gave Calum pause. Brix liked to top. Calum had known that years ago. And Calum preferred to bottom. Right? Or had he just done that more?

He knew the answer a week ago, but with Brix trembling in his arms, everything felt different. Calum kissed him, easing him onto his back, his heavier weight pinning him down. A dozen scenarios flashed through his head. He'd imagined this moment more times than he cared to admit, but never quite like this.

Brix was still shaking, breathing too fast.

Calum brushed his hair back from his face. "Can I fuck you?"

Brix exhaled hard. "I think I'll die if you don't."

"No dying." Calum reached for a condom. "Just bear with me—I haven't done this in years either."

He sat up to sheath his dick and grab the lube bottle.

Brix stole it—the bottle, not his dick—and flicked the cap. He slicked Calum's cock, and squeezed lube onto Calum's fingers. "I fucking need you."

"You have me." Calum let his fingers do the talking, working Brix up again, his dick a stone column of aching need.

Then he dropped a hand either side of Brix's head and let the stars align.

He slid inside Brix like he was made of glass, strong and pure—fragile—tracking every flutter and flicker in his face. Every shiver. Every breathless groan as he buried himself to the hilt.

"Fuck." Brix gripped Calum's shoulders. "You're so big."

"Am I hurting you?"

"No. *No*. It's just a lot."

"Breathe."

Brix obeyed, moving air through his lungs, relaxing around Calum's cock, his body taking over, drawing Calum deeper, coaxing him to thrust. And *thrust*, setting a rhythm that rolled their eyes and curled their toes, arching Brix's back from the bed.

Calum groaned, overcome, falling into it, as lost in Brix now as he'd always been. His kind heart and rough ways. His eyes, so haunted in the dark, but electric when he found the light. They moved together for what felt like hours. Dizzying pleasure entwined with a love Calum had never dreamed he'd find, as release bore down on him, on Brix too, sweet tension faltering the pace.

Wait for him.

Perhaps he always had been.

God, he's so beautiful.

Brix came a heartbeat before Calum, head thrown back, eyes screwed shut, a harsh groan tearing from his chest. A moment that, even if they never did this again, would be seared on Calum's soul forever.

I love him.

Eyes burning, he thrust deep and stayed there, pouring everything he had into Brix, forgetting about the condom, the meds, and the broken hearts that had steered them here. He forgot about everything except loving Brix.

And the fact that he was probably crushing the life out of him.

Oops.

He eased back, lifting his chest so Brix could breathe, and withdrew, catching the condom, poking it back in the wrapper to deal with later.

Sweat coated both of them. Calum gripped Brix's chin with a damp hand and searched his gaze for any sign of distress or regret.

He found none. Brix was dazed, but happy, his grin sleepy, but a mile wide, lighting the dim room as Calum stroked his cheek with the pad of his thumb. "All right?"

Brix nodded. "Can't find my tongue."

"I took it. It's mine."

"Fine by be." Brix's eyes started to close. Then they flew open, panic sparking as he seemed to notice the sticky mess between them for the first time.

His cum on Calum's skin.

"Fuck." He jerked up.

Calum restrained him. "Leave it."

"I—"

"Shh."

Brix didn't fight Calum.

Only himself.

Eventually, he fell asleep. But not for long, and the next time he opened his eyes they were clear. "Cal?"

"Yeah?"

"Will you fuck me again?"

EPILOGUE

SIX MONTHS LATER . . .

Brix woke to the first glimmer of sunshine they'd seen all week. He rolled over, his reaching hands found Calum, and like a moth to a flame, he chased Calum's warmth, wrapping himself around him until it was hard to tell where Calum ended and he began.

He dozed, drifting in and out of the best kind of sleep, but it was hard to stay in dreamland when his real dream come true was right there.

Calum was still sleeping. Brix propped himself up to stare, ghosting a fingertip over his cheekbone, lost in his mile-long dark lashes and velvet scruff. Calum had no idea how beautiful he was, but Brix knew it more and more every day they were together.

How did I get so lucky?

He'd asked the sea that a thousand times. Still didn't know. All he was certain of was that while watching Calum sleep had its perks, he *missed* him.

I need him.

Calum had a way of sensing disquiet in Brix before Brix did. His breathing changed and his eyes fluttered open, his slow and gentle smile wrapping Brix in sunshine. "Mornin'."

"Morning." Instant heat pooled in Brix's belly. He tried to hide it, but Calum knew him too well.

He tugged Brix on top of him, driving his morning wood against Brix's. "Were you lying in wait for me?"

"Maybe."

It was too early to fuck. They moved together instead, a languid, grinding rhythm that was almost as good as being buried in Calum's tight heat. That magical fucking thing Brix could almost do without blinking now.

They'd fucked last night. Calum on his knees, gripping the headboard, Brix driving into him from behind.

God.

"I'm gonna come," Calum suddenly gasped, cut off by the groan that tore through him. The deep shudder. *"Fuck."*

His release splattered his abdomen, Brix's too.

Reeling, Brix rose up and took himself in hand, leaning back, using Calum's strong thighs as support. A year ago, coming on someone had been filed so deep in his brain that he'd forgotten it was a thing.

With Calum, it was *every*-fucking-thing, and he didn't blink at that either. He came hard, and fast, watching his cum land on Calum's chest through hazy eyes.

Liberated.

Thankful.

Free.

They cleaned up. Calum cracked the lid of Brix's pill bottle and dropped what he needed in his palm. "Let's eat."

Calum had breakfast mastered. Brix had gained half a stone in the last six months and it felt amazing.

He inhaled everything Calum put in front of him. Then he took a shower, resisting the urge to drag Calum under the spray with him. Every morning was a fucking gift, but they had shit to do.

Chicken shit. Where it had all begun.

Calum drove, while Brix kicked back in the passenger seat. "Sure you don't want to take your dad instead of me? He seemed up for it when I saw him yesterday."

Brix choked on a laugh. "No chance. He'd get arrested again."

"You keep telling me shit like that, but your dad's so nice to me."

"He's mellowing in his old age."

"Are you? Rubi was telling me stories when I finished that chest piece last week."

"Rubi has a big mouth."

"He's big everywhere. Doesn't explain why you punched the old landlord of the Joker."

Fuck's sake. "This is what I get for introducing him to you?"

"So it's not true?"

"Of course it's true. Ain't the point. Tell *Rubi* I'll swap his appointments with Cam's and *he* can come to me. See how he likes to gossip while I'm the one with the needle."

Calum laughed. "Nice idea, but Rubi's the only biker from that club who digs dot work. The rest of them are all yours now Kim's not around much anymore."

"All but one."

"The quiet dude?"

"Saint Malone." Brix tapped his fingers on his bent knee. "I wasn't sure you'd noticed Lee sneaking him in after hours."

"I noticed. Just didn't think it was any of my business. That's her friend? From up north?"

"Yup. Small world, eh?"

"Depends what you're looking for." Calum spotted the sign for the battery farm and hung a left. "This is the place?"

"This is the shithole." Brix sat up and directed Calum up the narrow lane that led to the huge barn holding hundreds of hens. At first glance, the operation didn't look that bad—well-kept and tidy, with the right amount of homely touches. But Brix knew better. This farm was one of the worst he'd seen, and it made him wish the Rebel Kings Motorcycle Club cared as much about chickens as they did about fighting the Dog Crows up the road.

Calum parked. "What happens now?"

"We wait."

"How many are we taking?"

"As many as we can fit in the van."

"Fair enough. That the dude?" Calum pointed through Brix's window as the farmer emerged from the barn, dragging a handful of chickens by their legs, their heads scraping the ground. "What the fuck?"

Calum opened his door.

Brix grabbed him. "Be cool. Kicking off just makes it take longer."

"But—"

"Trust me. It's horrible, but we can't fix everything."

They got out of the van and approached the farmer, who greeted Brix with a curt nod. "How many?"

"Forty-five to start with. Might be able to squeeze in a few more."

"I've got seventy off to slaughter."

"We'll take as many as we can."

The farmer grunted, standing aside as Brix and Calum played Tetris with chicken crates until there was one left. A small one they could wedge on the front seat now Brix had a wingman to help him hold it steady.

Seventy birds.

Calum lifted the last crate over his head to take it to the farmer to be filled. In the early morning sun, his biceps bunched, displaying the black-and-grey lion Brix had etched for him before Christmas. His skin had been a dream to ink, and he carried the fact that he was the only soul to ever put a needle to Calum close to his heart.

The farmer threw the last birds in the crate. It was tough to watch, but Brix made himself do it, if only to remind himself why rescue runs were so important. Paying the farmer felt like rewarding him for being a complete cunt, but that was life—

A bird cried out, her leg caught in the crate's lid.

The farmer pushed down, oblivious, or not giving a fuck.

Brix moved to intervene, but the farmer shoved him away. "Ain't got time for your fuss this morning."

"Her leg's trapped. Lift the lid up."

"Piss *off.*"

The farmer pushed the lid again, and Brix saw red. Fury lit his veins, Lusmoore rage charging every step.

I'll kill him.

But his bunched fists never met their target. Cos Calum got there first.

The farmer fell on his arse, holding his jaw, stunned silent by the quiet man who'd morphed into the Incredible Hulk.

Brix sighed and tugged Calum away. "No more beer dates with my dad."

That day, thanks to Calum playing fast and loose with his fists, they found themselves with two-hundred more hens than they'd bargained for. Brix had to call his dad to build a giant new enclosure that took up every scrap of space in the garden.

Brix didn't seem sad about it. Calum had checked, more than once.

He hammered the last nail into the post, mindful of the Lusmoore audience watching him. "Will it hold all of them?"

John grunted, gruff and coarse. "If they're good gals. Could be rowdy if ya get a couple o' wrong'uns scrapping, but they'll settle down. Chooks can make a home anywhere."

"Thank fuck for that. Thought Brix might send me back to London when I told the farmer we'd pay double for his meat hens too."

"He'd have had me to answer to if he had." John rose from the damp grass. "Told him a hundred times that farmer wants shooting."

Calum couldn't disagree. By now, the Lusmoore way of thinking was life.

John left.

Calum had grand plans for sketching, but he felt the afternoon he'd spent away from Brix like it had been a week, a month, a year.

Miss him.

He walked to the shop. Brix was tattooing one of the bikers, the blond one who smiled a lot and had the same habit as Rubi of falling asleep on the table.

The quiet gave Brix space to concentrate, head down, lip caught between his teeth. If not for his longer hair and new geometric knuckle tattoos, they could've been in Camden a decade ago.

His face is just the same.

But was it? Back then, Calum had missed the black emotions that had almost taken Brix from the world forever.

He didn't miss them now, and he moved closer, stepping into Brix's eye-line. "All right?"

Brix wiped blood from the biker's skin, as if it took him a second to believe Calum was real. Then he smiled and Calum relaxed.

He's okay.

"I missed you," Brix mouthed.

Calum grinned and blew him a kiss.

Then he retreated to the desk to do all the shit no one got round to now Lena was gone, and it was late by the time he glanced up to see the biker leaving the shop.

He felt Brix's presence behind him like an open oven door. Made himself wait for the slow slide of Brix's arms around him. "How did it go today?"

Brix kissed Calum's neck. "With what?"

"With Kim."

"How do you think it went?" Brix turned the kiss into a bite. "It was fucking fine and the only thing he was bothered about was that I hadn't told him years ago."

Calum shut the computer down and turned to face Brix. "Don't feel bad about that. You told him when you were ready. Do you think you'll tell anyone else?"

"I told Cam. Dropped it on him while I was inking him before Nash."

"Cam O'Brian?" Calum tilted his head, picturing the president of the motorcycle club that seemed to have brothers everywhere he looked now summer was here. "Why him? I didn't know you were that close."

"We're not. But we've known each other a long time—I

trust him—and I wanted to see what it was like to tell someone I've inked a thousand times."

"How was it?"

Brix took a slow breath. "Amazing, actually. Deep down, I know I was scared he'd react badly, but he was so fucking nice. Almost made me cry."

Emotion welled in Calum too, and he wasn't ashamed to show it. "I'm happy for you. Are you ready to go?"

"Always ready for you, mate."

The innuendo made Calum hot all over. Sex with Brix was a wild, complex thing that kept him on his toes every day of the week. Every night.

God, I love him.

And he always would.

Thank you so much for reading House of Cards! I hope you enjoyed Brix and Calum's love story.

And, of course, it doesn't end there. Kim has his own book in Junkyard Heart. And if you're interested in the Rebel Kings MC, the entire series is available to binge on Kindle Unlimited. And yes, Rubi, Cam, Nash, and Saint are so worth it.

Brix and Calum also have bonus scenes on my Patreon.

Find my whole catalogue on my Amazon page!